# Different Shades of Dreams

BreAnn Hanks

# Hanks Publishing
Publishing Co.

Follow us, Hanks Publishing, on Instagram!



Cover art and Book Design by BreAnn hanks
Edition 2

# Prologue

Raja leaps onto the flat surface of Jarom's landing area and starts for the opening of his cave.

She's impatient. She knows what he's doing, but her companion will *never* be completely ready for the role. They need her guidance!

Raja is not going to live for much longer!

Klauss, her companion's best friend, joins her flank, letting her know that he's here for the same reason. His fingertips brush her side, making her lightly growl at the sparks of energy that run through her. She most definitely could use the boost right now. Her bones are aging, making her sore with each trek she makes here.

At the opening, Raja and Klauss hear the mighty beast from inside speak up.

"She is not ready," Jarom says from deep inside of his cave.

"Well, she's going to have to be," Klauss calls out as he and Raja enter. "It's time."

"You think I'm going to let Kera out?" Jarom scoffs in disdain. "You know what she did."

"She'll eventually pay for her crimes. And my best friend knows the *best* punishment for her."

Raja growls in agreement, her tail slashing from side to side.

"Raja, I don't recall you having a say in this," Jarom grumbles.

"She has every say," Klauss snaps. "And right! Bring my best friend here or I will ask Amelia to do it!"

"Amelia is no better than her mother." Jarom retorts.

"Nor is Alia and look at her! You let her prance around and do whatever she wants!" Klauss shakes his head, Raja growling in disapproval this time.

Witches…

They think they run this world. They think they're gods! Raja's companion would *never* approve of this!

"He would never approve! Nor my best friend!"

"Then what do you suggest I do?" Jarom slithers his head out like a snake, Raja watching him shift his weight. "Let Kera out and let her cast her spells, again? You know damn well what would happen if I did that."

"Earthquakes," Klauss agrees. "Twice a day. Every single day. Until we cease to exist in thirteen days."

"Each earthquake would be worse than the last. We *don't*. Want her to feel the tearing in her heart. It will kill her."

"As with Raja and me. You *know* we're connected to her."

Jarom goes quiet and Raja watches him. He's hesitant. She can smell the fear on him. She doesn't blame him where Kera nearly killed him almost a decade ago when he and Raja trapped Kera in prison.

"Jarom," Klauss snaps, again. "She needs. To take care. Of us. She has matters to attend to!"

"Like what?" Jarom grumbles.

"Like what," Klauss repeats in discernment, keeping a cool tone. "What about Lillian? The Black Cat? She hasn't been able to see her family for *ten years!* And don't get me started about the spell that none of the witches will break without her here! They think they can run this world! We need. Amari. Here." Klauss points down at the ground as he keeps eye contact with Jarom.

Jarom looks at Raja. "Raja? Is this how you feel as well?"

Raja shows her teeth in a growl, in favor of her companion's best friend.

"Fine." Jarom pulls his head back in the shadows, but he forgets Raja can see him. "I'll take care of it."

"Thank you." Klauss starts for the opening.

"Oh, and Klaussof."

"What?" Klauss snaps a little before stopping and realizing his mistake, looking back at Jarom.

"Don't corner me, again. You might not be so lucky next time."

Raja roars at Jarom and grows to her battle size, protecting Klauss. *You will not threaten my companion's best friend! One wrong move and I will tear you to shreds!*

Oh, how Raja wishes Jarom could hear her thoughts and not just see her threat. She will *not* let him threaten the innocent! He knows damn well she can kill him easily! All he's got to do is look at his wing he can't use anymore!

Jarom went after Klauss once before and Raja reminded the dragon the cost of crime no matter the sort.

Jarom dips his head at Raja as he remembers, backing off. She may not be as big as him at her battle size, but she's faster than him on foot, having the advantage since she grounded him.

Raja fluffs out her fur to look bigger and meaner, backing out of the cave slowly as she watched Klauss's back. Once outside she slowly shrinks back down and lowers her fur.

Klauss sets his hand on her back. "Thank you," he starts, sounding grateful for such a protective friend. "Raja. I honestly don't know what I would do without you."

Raja presses her forehead into Klauss's side and looks up at him lovingly. She may be a wild animal like Jarom and understands where he's coming from. But she would *never* hurt anyone of this world.

# 1

Amari breathes out as she comes up from a squat. Is she doing this right? Breathe in when you go down… And out as you come up?

Amari doesn't really work out. She just does squats whenever she needs to stretch out her thighs and butt. And because she does it so much, her ass looks great! Her mind elsewhere she does her best not to smile like a fool. Being with Garrett last night sparked a new flame inside of her, giving her hope.

It's been three months since Mike left and Erika's wedding is just around the corner. Amari can't believe how long it's been since the break-up. And she's still in love with Mike. He cheated on her with Madi then dropped everything and left when Madi cheated on him with his brother. He deserved it. After Amari and Mike were together for ten years! They almost got pregnant a couple times!

Adam walks into the kitchen and gets a beer from the fridge. Amari watches him in disbelief, but she continues to do her squats. Adam closes the fridge, opens his beer, and starts drinking it. He looks at her with his beer in the air and pressed against his lips, his head thrown back.

Uh oh. She knows that look. What is she doing wrong this time? Adam slowly puts his beer down and turns to face Amari, letting out a breath from chugging his beer. He sets his beer down on the island, his eyes on her as she continues her squats.

"You're doing it wrong," Adam puts in, judging Amari's squats.

"Enlighten me," Amari teases.

"In when you come up. Out when you go down."

Amari nods her head. She switches her breathing as if she's changed her demeanor with ease. She quickly breathes out as she goes down in a squat and breathes in as she comes up. She continues to stretch her thighs and butt, Adam watching her. They're best friends. And they have been close since they were just four years old.

Adam takes a noticeable breath. "You know." He grabs his beer and starts for Amari, walking around the island with farmhouse gray cupboards and a white marble vanity top with the sink in the middle.

Adam clears his throat and Amari knows he's about to use his authoritative tone on her. "I can be your personal trainer."

Amari watches Adam. "You know I'm not interested."

"Amari."

"Adam," Amari drawls out. "I don't work out. You know this."

Adam stands right in front of Amari as she continues to do her squats, watching her. Her eyes meet with his every time she comes up from a squat. "But you squat like you do. I mean… You do this daily!"

"I sit most of the day because of my job. This feels good."

Adam giggles, watching Amari. "Yet you still look very attractive with no fat on your body."

Amari glares at Adam as she comes up from a squat. He's hitting on her?! That's new! Especially, when he's married with a child! Adam clears his throat and changes his demeanor.

"Sorry." Adam tosses his dirty blond bangs back. "Has he…"

Amari looks at Adam as she continues her squats. "Has who done what?"

"So, he hasn't come by."

"Who?"

"Mike."

Amari stands right in front of Adam, staring at him in shock as she forgets about her stretches. "What?"

Adam searches Amari's eyes, sober.

"He's back?"

Adam nods his head. "Yeah," he replies softly.

"I need to." Amari trails off and grabs her bag from the chair.

"Mare," Adam starts, trailing off and grabbing her attention.

Amari stops at the front door and looks back at her best friend that's always been there for her, even through the break-up. Her brown eyes meet Adam's green eyes.

"He's changed… Be careful."

Amari nods her head and walks out of the house, grabbing the keys to her truck.

∞

Mike drinks his bourbon then puts his empty glass down. At Mim's Bar and Grill, he's only in his hometown for a short while. His mom's wedding.

After his dad passed away when Mike was just sixteen it took a while for his family to truly move on. His mom started dating five years later and she's finally getting married to her boyfriend of ten years. Fifteen years since Mike's dad's passing… It's still tough to get through.

Mike's dad was tough, but he had a loving side that taught Mike how to treat women no matter how toxic they are. But if you were to ask Madi, Mike's last girlfriend, she would say he's toxic and doesn't know any better. He heard rumors that she talks bad about him. Mike acknowledges the bartender, his best friend, as the bartender pours him a glass of whiskey.

"Congratulations," Chris mumbles. "Your ex is going to kill you."

"I wouldn't be surprised," Mike says with a low growl. "My mom absolutely loves her." Mike throws the whiskey down his throat, the burn almost nothing compared to Amari's rage.

He sets the glass down and looks at Chris as Chris pours a glass of beer from the tap for a man that's starting to get a buzz.

"What do you think she's going to say first?" Mike watches his best friend.

"You're an idiot," Chris replies.

"You're an idiot," a familiar female voice snaps as she approaches Mike, repeating Chris. She looks at him. "Hey, Chris."

Chris looks at Amari. "Hey, Mare." He acknowledges her before giving the beer to the buzzed man at the bar.

"I was your girlfriend for what?" Amari starts, standing next to Mike as she gets in between him and the empty chair next to him. Fuck… This wasn't going to end well and Mike can't do anything about it. "Almost ten years?"

"Amari." Knowing better than to look at her when she's angry, Mike keeps his head low. "I'm sorry. But you're not the easiest to just ask to be my date to a wedding."

"It's your mom's wedding. She personally delivered the invitation to my door. And she wants me to walk down the aisle on your arm. So, you better patch it up with me before the big day."

Chris hands Amari a bottled water and she thanks him, taking it. Mike pushes his stool back and stands up. He puts down a tip for Chris then looks at Amari, not wasting any more time.

"I'm sorry," Mike replies, his brown eyes meeting Amari's brown eyes. "For cheating on you. And making you look like an idiot in front of Madi."

"My own cousin. You cheated on me with my own cousin."

"Well, she…"

Amari cuts Mike off. "Don't start."

Mike sighs and sags. "She fell away like I did. We connected."

Amari glares at Mike in disbelief. ""Just like how a stud connects with a mare," she mumbles sarcastically. Amari shakes her head. "I was there for you and your family when your dad passed away," she snaps, sounding heartbroken. "His passing didn't just break your guys' hearts. It also broke mine."

"Amari, if you can just understand."

"I was just as close to him as you were!" Amari cuts Mike off.

He winces. He knows that. He knows how close Amari and his dad were. He always suspected that she was cheating on him with his dad. But he could never prove it. And when he broke it off with Madi a few months ago he found out *she* was cheating on him with his brother.

Mike shudders. He gives into Amari, knowing just the way to turn all of this around. He grabs her hip and pulls her into him for a hug, looking at her.

"I'm sorry," he whispers. "I just thought since Madi…"

"I'm *nothing* like Madi," Amari warns with a growl, glaring up at Mike. "I'm in love with you, Mike. I would *never*. Have an affair with anyone."

"I thought you were," Mike mutters. He searches Amari's eyes, looking for any sign of empathy.

She lost her dad to prostate cancer when it was caught too late. And Mike was there for her. Amari's dad was hard on her and her siblings, but he loved them. He just had a funny way of showing it when they were just kids. In Amari and Mike's twenties her dad started to come around and made it up to her and her siblings all through her early twenties until he passed away.

Amari shakes her head, her brown eyes looking dim in the lighting. "Your dad treated me like a daughter. No more."

Mike sighs and sags heavily. He rests his chin on Amari's shoulder as he holds her close. "I love you," he breathes softly near her ear.

Amari sighs with a growl. "Don't disappear like that, again," she threatens through her teeth. "You just about gave your mom a heart attack."

Mike nods his head as he rubs Amari's back and gives her a squeeze. "I'm sorry," he whispers.

"Sorry isn't enough." Amari shoves Mike off of her, throws back a shot that she catches as Chris slides it down to her, then walks out the front door.

∞

Madi runs past the sheep as she gets her morning run in. She used to be a soccer player and she goes running every morning to keep herself in shape. She doesn't play soccer anymore since her knee injury a few years back. The doctor told her no.

Madi jumps over a great pyrenees that's guarding the sheep she passes and she hears him barking. She feels his hot breath on her ankles and she pushes harder, not wanting to get caught. She outruns the dog after a few paces and he loses interest. Madi jumps over a dead tree. Landing hard, a stabbing pain sets in her knee. She stops for a second to take a breather and sits on the dead wood. That's when she recognizes her surroundings. She's in her backyard.

She starts to wonder if her mom is back from swimming at the natatorium and that's when a male hand extends in front of her. Rage sets in when she looks up to see it's her cousin's best friend. Madi stands up and swats Adam's hand aside.

"I don't need your help," Madi mutters. She starts for the house.

"I just came here to warn you," Adam puts in as he follows Madi.

"Warn? Or threaten? Cause you've done plenty of that!"

"A little bit of both," Adam replies after a moment of silence. Did he have to think about that? "Madi. Stop. Let's talk."

"No." Madi opens the sliding screen door on the back of the house then she opens the sliding door.

"We need to talk."

"About what?" Madi steps inside and closes the door on Adam, looking at him through the window with a sly grin.

He opens the door once she starts walking away. "Your cousin."

"You mean your best friend?"

"Yes," Adam snaps, hard on Madi's tail. "My best friend who happens to be your cousin!"

"Not after her last threat towards me."

"Mike cheated on her with you. What do you expect?"

"Well, I disowned her." Madi starts up the stairs and Adam follows. "So, you don't have to worry about it."

"Your side of your family is so dysfunctional y'all need to go through boot camp to learn respect." Adam spats, sounding mad and irritated.

"Wiley did."

"And look how he turned out."

"No comment."

Adam follows Madi into her bedroom and watches her as she pulls her t-shirt over her head and reveals her sports bra. "Look. Amari is going to Mike's mom's wedding. And I don't want you to interfere."

Madi looks over at Adam. "We're in Wellsville. Why would I go to Corinne for a stupid wedding?"

"I just wanna make sure you don't have any plans coming to crash a wedding you're not invited to."

Madi gets rid of her pants and throws them into the dirty clothes basket, her eyes still on the man she once had a relationship with years ago. They would still be together if it wasn't for Amari. "Like you said. I'm not invited."

"Good. Sounds like Eric made a good decision."

*I wouldn't go that far,* Madi thinks to herself.

Truthfully, she's going to the wedding. Eric asked her to walk down the aisle with him. They don't care that his mom doesn't want her there. They're going as a couple and bridesmaid and groomsmen. It's their plan and they're sticking to it.

"Don't do anything stupid," Adam threatens low as if he can read Madi's mind.

His comment throws her off and she tries to cover up her stumble by acting like her shoes that she kicked off got in the way.

"It's not your fuckin' wedding. It's my best friend's mom."

Madi glares at Adam. How does he know what she's planning?! And since when has Mike been Adam's best friend? Last Madi knew, Mike and Adam fell apart after getting in a fight over Amari's welfare! The day Adam and Amari walked in on Mike and Madi doing the deed. If they didn't interrupt, Mike would've spilt his seed inside of Madi instead of on her stomach.

"I don't plan on going," Madi lies through her teeth, a glare telling Adam 'Get the fuck out of my house'.

He turns his back to her and starts for the door as she takes her bra off. "Then learn some decency, Madison." Adam threatens. He thrusts the door closed behind him, slamming it.

"You used to see me naked all the time, Adam!"

"Fuck you, Madison!" Well, that was rude! "And you're the rude one!" Adam's yell is heard down the hall. How did he know?!

Madi shakes her head and tries to shake off the weirdness that she just witnessed. What was that all about? Is Adam in her head somehow? Madi tries to forget the confrontation, taking her panties off and then starting for the shower.

She grabs her towel and wraps it around her body as she walks through her bedroom door and to the bathroom. She swears she hears a music box, but none of her family has one.

Madi can't believe Adam! He sticks up for Amari as if she needs protecting! He treats *her* like a queen. A goddess! While he treats Madi like she's the devil! Other than having an affair with Mike what did she do to get this kind of treatment! Everyone has moved on from that fiasco! At least, Madi thought!

Madi locks herself in the bathroom and turns the shower on. As she waits for the water to heat up, she washes her face in the sink. She's been told she needs to apologize to Amari. And while she loves her cousin, her cousin needs to learn it's not all about her. And part of the reason why Madi disowned Amari is because Amari thought Mike should revolve around her. Well, it's about time for Madi to be revolved around. Mike, Adam, and Amari should appreciate her and treat her like the queen *she* is!

Madi dries her face with her towel then lets the towel fall down to the floor. Her slim, but sporty figure shows off her curves and big thighs, her breasts not entirely small or huge either, round and plump. Her skin fair, Madi looks like she's of Native American descent. But she has no desire to find out if she actually is. All of her family is white, not showing a sign of Native American descent.

Madi steps into the shower and makes sure it's scorching hot. She wants her worries to melt away like a Scentsy melt wax in a wax warmer. And while she washes her body and hair, she gets that moment. Madi doesn't give a care in the world as she showers. She wants nothing to do with this world! If she could have her own world, she would take care of it and make sure no one like Amari could enter it.

Madi lets the scorching hot water fall down on her until it turns icy cold. She wants to stay in the shower, but she does have a wedding to get ready for. Madi turns the shower off and steps out, pulling the shower curtain back. She dries herself off then lightly combs her hair. She puts curl enhancing foam in her hair, brushing it through the strands of her hair with her fingers. Madi doesn't use this stuff much, but when she does it makes her curls bounce with life.

Madi puts her hair in a French braid starting at the very top of her head. It takes her an hour to get every strand of hair in the braid in turn. But she gets it done nonetheless and puts a hair tie in the bottom of the braid.

Madi wraps her towel around her body then walks out of the bathroom and to her bedroom. She hears the music playing from a music box, again, but she dismisses it, shaking her head. That's just odd. Why is there music playing?

Madi gets in her room and closes the door behind her. She can't have any distractions right now. She needs to get ready! And let everyone know that she's the star of the show! Not Eric's mom! Madi grabs her lotion and puts some on her left leg, propping it up on the chest at the foot of her bed. She lathers it and rubs the lotion in. Her legs silky smooth from shaving last night, Madi is ready for Eric to take her tonight. She loves how rough he is and how he loves her. They've only been together for a few months, but it feels like they've been together for longer.

Madi puts her left foot down and props her right foot on the chest. She lathers her right leg with lotion and rubs it in. Madi makes sure she rubs extra on the knot that she has in her calf. She goes to a masseuse after a long hard day at work and it feels nice. She needs to go tomorrow for her knots in her back and legs. She's been adding a lot of stress to them.

Madi puts her leg down on the floor and walks over to her closet. She grabs her red wine mummy wrap dress and her black pumps. She tosses them onto her made bed as she walks over to her dresser. It doesn't take long for her to find her lace panties and she slides them on with ease. She grabs her dress from the bed and admires it. Since Eric's mom won't give Madi a bridesmaid dress, Madi went out after finding out the colors and found her a dress. The red wine is a good color on her and compliments her skin color. She just couldn't pass up the opportunity on the color and style of dress. She's going to look like a goddess!

Madi lets her towel fall down to the floor and she puts the dress on. She puts her black pumps on and then reaches back to zip her dress up. Male hands interrupt Madi's pulling on the zipper as music from a music box starts playing in her room. She sighs with relief. He's here early!

"Thank you," Madi replies. "I needed that."

"You're welcome," a male voice Madi doesn't recognize says low. She stiffens. Wait… This isn't Eric!

Madi turns around to face the man. He stands at six feet and two inches and he looks like he stepped out of another world, his handsome features similar to Adam's. "Wait. Who are you?"

The man smiles devilishly. "Your worst nightmare," he growls before grabbing Madi's wrist and taking her with him through her bedroom mirror. The man lets go of Madi and she trips.

Madi falls on her side with a thud and the wind gets knocked out of her lungs. She clenches her eyes shut in pain and rolls onto her back. Fuck, that hurt! Why did that hurt so much? Madi tries to catch her breath as a couple people stand over her.

"Are you sure this isn't her," a woman asks. "I'm positive," the man that pulled Madi through her mirror says. "This is the one he told me to grab. It's not. Her."

"Yeah, but. She should be here. Plus, look at this one. She's dressed like a goddess!"

"But this isn't our goddess. This is the next in line that needs discipline. Just like he asked."

The woman sighs. "You better be right."

"Of course, I'm right! Have I ever been wrong?"

The woman goes quiet.

"Don't answer that."

Madi looks up at the man and woman, none of them familiar to her. "Who are you?"

"It's not her," the woman replies.

"Totally," the man replies.

# 2

Amari smooths her red wine country belle dress down, waiting her turn to walk down the aisle with her small bouquet of white lilies, dark red dahlias, silver dollar eucalyptus, and ruscus.

The silk tube top of Amari's bridesmaid dress is covered in lace, the lace turning into a halter top with a turtleneck around the neck. The country belle skirt is silk with lace over it, lightly blending into the silk. Amari absolutely loves this dress! And the bouquets for the three bridesmaids are absolutely perfect.

Amari was happy to help Erika, Mike's mom, to plan the wedding with her two soon to be stepdaughters. Kylee and CeeCee are great helpers and absolutely beautiful. And they absolutely love Erika.

Amari steps forward as the oldest of the bridesmaids meets with her brother, who is the oldest of the groomsmen, and the brother and sister walk down the aisle with their arms locked. Amari looks back at the youngest daughter as she pulls on Amari's dress.

"It was tucked into your panties," CeeCee whispers.

Amari snorts and laughs quietly, covering her mouth with her hand. "It's been a while since I've worn just panties," she whispers.

CeeCee nods her head. "I only wear them when I'm on my period."

Amari laughs quietly. "Garments get stained way too easily."

CeeCee nods her head in agreement then Amari looks at Mike, who looks her up and down as if he's love stricken. But he has no idea the battle Amari is dealing with on the inside. She wants him. But then she doesn't.

He broke her heart. And she doesn't know if she can ever trust him, again. Amari steps forward and meets him in the middle. He offers her his arm and she gladly takes it. They walk slowly to the music, letting the song play out.

"You look absolutely beautiful," Mike whispers.

"Thank you," Amari whispers. "So does your mom."

"I saw her before this. She couldn't have picked a more beautiful dress. Thank you."

"She's like a second mother to me. I couldn't look the other way."

"You've helped her a lot. And I appreciate it."

Amari nods her head and looks down as it goes quiet between them. She and Mike split at the end of the aisle after a moment, where the bishop of their ward is waiting. Amari stands next to Kylee with her bouquet in hand.

Kylee leans in standing just an inch taller than Amari and speaks in Amari's ear.

"You and Mike look so cute together," Kylee whispers.

"Thank you," Amari whispers, her heart screaming for this conversation to end right where it is. She looks up at Kylee.

"I heard what happened. And I am so. So sorry. CeeCee went through the same thing but with her best friend. Let's just say her best friend is lucky to be alive."

Amari snorts and bites back a laugh, pulling her lips into her mouth and lightly biting them. She feels the same way about her cousin!

"The guy isn't, though. Our brother got to him before I could."

"Most of my family sides with me. Mike broke all of our hearts. Not just mine."

Kylee makes a sound in disgust. "That's why women are better," she says lowly.

"I totally agree," Amari mutters, letting Kylee know that she's not exactly straight. Amari used to be straight. But when she turned twenty, she started to realize her attraction to men *and* women wasn't normal. Amari has kept her sexuality preference to herself for ten years, knowing that her family would shun her and disown her. She doesn't want that.

Mike has known Amari's sexuality preference before she even figured it out herself. He always encouraged her to date women and she's been getting out of her bubble a little bit. She's gone on a couple dates with two different women and they went okay. But the women had some red flags that made Amari decide not to take them out, again. And she's stuck to her word.

CeeCee joins Amari on her right and leans into her to get something off of her boot. Amari looks down to realize CeeCee forgot to take one of the tags off. Amari snorts and holds back a laugh, a smile on her face. She did that at her cousin's wedding a couple years ago! He was getting married to his high school sweetheart after being together for eight years.

At the wedding, Amari was sitting down next to her mom when her oldest brother grabbed a tag that was still on her cardigan from behind. They had a good laugh at the same time the bishop said "Speak now or forever hold your peace." That's a memory everyone will remember.

Amari presses her lips together as she has that flashback, not wanting to ruin the moment. She succeeds to stop her giggling fit and get right back into the tender mood for the wedding.

The music changes and Erika walks down the aisle in her beautiful off-white country belle dress similar to the bridesmaids' dresses. The only difference is the rose gold lace turning into sleeves, an add-on Erika so desperately wanted. She absolutely loves lace and just wanted more of it. People stay on their feet as Garrett, Erika's brother, looks at Amari and their eyes meet.

Amari still hasn't forgotten everything that he's done for her, stepping in when Mike cheated on her and her dad wasn't around to beat the shit out of Mike. Garrett is an amazing father. But he's also just amazing in general. He's such a good man and he deserves a good woman that will give him the world.

Garrett kisses Erika's cheek as they reach the end of the aisle then hands her off to her future husband. He glances at Amari and gives her a wink, reminding her of last night. Again, Amari bites back a laugh, pressing her lips together and just giving Garrett a flirtatious wink.

She'll have a chat with him later.


∞


Mike pulls Amari aside, taking her into the women's bathroom. At the luncheon, Mike took the moment to grab Amari before she could sit next to Garrett, who's been eyeing her like she's a piece of candy.

"What the hell is that," Mike asks softly.

"What the hell is what," Amari asks, not entertained by Mike's rudeness.

"You know what." Mike snaps.

Amari narrows her eyes at Mike and a toilet flushes. They wait patiently as Mike's now stepcousin comes out of the bathroom stall and washes her hands. Amari lifts an eyebrow, challenging Mike to start something in front of family.

He ignores the challenge and stares at her coolly. He puts his hands in his front pockets and waits patiently as his stepcousin takes her time to check for pimples in the bathroom mirror and pop a couple. What is she trying to do? Save Amari from humiliation? That's just great! Maybe Mike should've taken Amari into the men's bathroom. At least that way the men would've gotten the fuck out so they didn't get in the crossfire or just to be respectful!

Mike's stepcousin walks in between him and Amari, but he keeps his eyes on Amari as his stepcousin sets her hand on Amari's arm and gives her a reassuring squeeze before walking out of the bathroom.

"Anybody else in here," Mike asks, speaking up.

A woman is heard saying "fuck" then she flushes the toilet. Wait a second… Mike knows that voice! His now stepsister walks out of the bathroom stall and quickly washes her hands. A woman follows her from the same bathroom stall and washes her hands in the sink next to Kylee.

Great… Mike just interrupted play time for Kylee in an LDS church bathroom. That's going to be an awkward conversation for later!

Kylee holds her head up high as she takes her partner's hand in her hand and they walk out of the bathroom together. Mike waits a moment then he starts for the bathroom stalls, noticing one is closed. Amari steps forward and cuts him off.

"I'll get it," Amari threatens low. She walks over to the stall that has the door closed and she knocks on it. "It's safe to come out," Amari says softly.

No response. Amari gets in the open stall next to the one with the closed door and stands on the top of the toilet to look in. She gets down from the toilet instantly and shakes her head. She pushes on the closed door, but it doesn't open. Amari sighs and sags. Some little one must've locked it and couldn't get it unlocked.

Amari walks over to Mike and crosses her arms, glaring at him. "Talk," she says lowly.

"You and Garrett," Mike snaps lowly, treading lightly since he knows that tone of voice. It's a dangerous one from any woman!

Amari is ready to kill and she's not thrilled with Mike's questioning. "There's nothing between us."

"Bullshit. Back there. During the ceremony. And just now! He's looking at you like you're a York peppermint patty ready to be eaten!"

"We ran into each other last night."

"What'd you do? Eat each other out?"

Amari snaps and shoves Mike into the wall hard. She slaps him in the face and gets dangerously close to him. "My sex life has nothing to do with you. Michael. And if you wanna be able to have kids, I suggest you nip the conversation here and now."

Mike looks at Amari's lips. "I want kids… But with you."

Amari shoves Mike in the chest. "You lost that privilege when you slept with my cousin." She threatens. She's not playing games and Mike is dangerously close to pressing her buttons for a full-on attack.

Mike kisses Amari and she closes up on him. She shoves him off of her and grabs onto the lapel of his jacket, panting. He knows what she's thinking. And he beats himself up for it all the time.

"I miss you," Mike whispers. He lets his forehead rest on Amari's forehead and he tucks her bangs behind her ear, his fingertips brushing her temple. "And I want you back."

"Mike, don't," Amari threatens with a growl, shaking her head. "Don't give me hope."

Mike puts his lips to Amari's forehead, wanting her to give into him. But he knows it will take time. "I made a mistake. And it will *never*. Happen again."

The women's bathroom door opens and Amari pushes Mike off of her. He looks at her to see she's breaking inside all over again. No! He doesn't want to break her heart! He wants to mend it! Help it heal! A man clears his throat and Mike looks at his uncle. Fuck. Any uncle but him! Why does it have to be him?

"Mike, your mother is looking for you," Garrett says. His gray eyes look sincere. "She needs to talk to you about the cows. There's been an incident."

Mike nods his head and Garrett slips aside, holding the door open for his nephew. Mike slips out and looks for his mom. When there's an incident on the farm you need to leave right away, no matter what you're doing.

But Mike doesn't have the keys to his truck. His mom took them from him this morning when he came home drunk last night. She didn't want him visiting the bar on her wedding day. But now she's got to give his keys back to him. Mike finds his mom and sneaks his hand on her bare back. He puts his lips to her ear, standing behind her.

"Keys, please," Mike says.

Erika turns around to look at her beloved son. "Cow got stuck in the feeder." She pulls Mike's keys out from underneath her breast in her dress. "Again. Same one."

Mike sighs in disappointment. "That one's going to be for dinner tomorrow."

"I hope you like it bruised." Erika teases. Mike snorts. Erika puts Mike's truck keys in his extended hand. "Go take care of her. And don't go to the bar after. You're helping Amari take the decorations down tonight once your stepfather and I are gone."

Mike nods his head. "Yes, ma'am." He kisses Erika's cheek. "Congratulations, Momma. And happy birthday."

"Thank you."

Mike pulls away from his beloved mom and starts out the church.

∞

Garrett looks at Amari and their eyes meet. Her brown hair half-up and half-down with curls and low-lights she looks like a goddess.

Her brown eyes pop out from her red wine dress. Amari's silver earrings dangle from her ears like icicles, moving only when she turns her head. Amari looks at Garrett with the same broken heart from a few months ago.

"Amari, I'm so sorry," Garrett whispers softly. "I should've known."

"He caught your looks towards me," Amari says low and softly. "He thinks we're together."

"As he should." Garrett walks into the women's bathroom and pulls Amari into a hug. She buries her face into his chest. "You're absolutely beautiful, Mare. And every man is going to look at you the same way I do. I mean… You lost almost eighty pounds in just three months. It's insane!"

Amari sighs and sags. Her hands fall down Garrett's back and she looks up at him. "All thanks to a stupid man."

"That stupid man doesn't deserve you," Garrett says low. He brushes Amari's temple with the tip of his fingers, his gray eyes on her brown eyes. He can really see her green rings around the brown pop out. It's time. He can tell. "You deserve much better."

At only fifteen years apart, Garrett can make a move on Amari if he truly desired. He's the youngest in his family and only married when he got his ex-wife pregnant at the age of sixteen. It didn't last for much longer after she had their son and he didn't feel anything for her.

But with Amari… Garrett has watched her grow up and when she turned fifteen, she confessed her feelings to Mike. That's when they became a couple. It started with the couple just kissing and holding hands. When they turned sixteen, Mike started to take Amari on dates in his new mustang. But when he got home from his mission in Ireland, they consummated their love for each other his first night back home.

Garrett spent some time with Amari while Mike was on his mission. And then he's had Amari to himself the last three months. Garrett would do anything to mend her broken heart. He cares for Amari greatly. He loves her. But he knew he couldn't have her forever. He could never hurt Viggo that way.

Amari searches Garrett's gray eyes and he lets his forehead rest on her forehead. He wants to kiss her. But he doesn't want to kiss her when she's not ready. Amari wraps her arms around Garrett's neck and he kisses her cheek. He pulls her into him, tightening his hug on her reassuringly.

"You've been amazing," Amari says softly. "Thank you."

"Anything for you, Amari," Garrett says softly.

"Can I be honest with you?"

"Always."

"Sometimes I hate this world. I just wish… Sometimes I wish there's another world waiting for me. Like I'm their…" Amari sighs and relaxes into Garrett. "I don't know. *Chosen one*," Amari says in a low voice.

Garrett snorts and stifles a laugh. "Wanna know something crazy?"

"What?"

"There is another world. That your grandfather created."

Amari pulls back and lets her hands rest on Garrett's shoulders, staring at him in disbelief.

"And they're all waiting for you. Their goddess."

"Don't toy with me, Garrett," Amari warns lowly.

"Amari Rose Greenwood," Garrett starts formally, his hands on Amari's hips. "Daughter of Christopher Lee Greenwood and granddaughter of Nolan Lane Billow… I pronounce you. As the rightful heir. Of Hallam."

Amari lets out a breath she was holding in and tears form in her eyes.

"You may now get to shift between Homba and Hallam anytime you like."

Amari holds Garrett's face in her hands and her lips land on his lips.

∞

Raja looks up from her nest and she softly growls in celebration.

He did it! He made Amari the official heir of Hallam! Now, she can cross over and get crowned! This is a *huge* celebration that must be had! If Amari chooses wisely, she will have a god on her side that will protect her and be with her through thick and thin. She's got so many good choices! And while her heart is with her officiant, she still has a lot of good men to choose from here in Hallam.

Garrett will be coming back for the crowning and he's a great pick as he cares for this world as he would care for his own children.

Viggo is another good pick as well. He fought in the war against Kera and made sure his men and women that were chosen for the war stayed safe. He's strong, caring, loyal, cunning, and smart. Viggo is a hunter and he only kills to survive. He has an appreciation for all life in this world and is Garrett's equal. It's a good thing they're good friends.

Klauss is also a good pick. He's quick on his feet and he's always ten steps ahead, planning every battle and how each one can go. He always plans every single outcome, not wanting to be scurrying for a new plan if it doesn't go his way the first time. Or the second time. His love and appreciation for Amari is rare as well. Even though they're just best friends, they could most definitely be the couple that cares for each other greatly.

Raja gets up and walks out of her nest as she scents one of her sons nearby. He's got news and she wants to meet him in the middle. It's time to plan a wedding. And a crowning. Everything must go accordingly. Madi will try to get in the way once she catches the news of Amari being the official heir of this world.

Raja meets Raheim out in the entry of the quarters and they rub foreheads. She saved him when he was just a cub. His mother was shot by a poacher and he and his sister were left behind for lions or hyenas to find them. Raja found them before harm could fall upon them.

Raheim rubs his head on Raja's shoulder and nips her side playfully. Raja moans at him and snaps her teeth at him, not in the mood to play.

"News," Raja says with her body language.

Raheim looks at her and his bronze eyes meet her evergreen eyes. "Madison just heard." He growls. "She's not very happy."

"Who told her?" Raja growls.

"Lord Brothwell."

"Her lover. Of course." Raja growls in annoyance and frustration. She knew this would happen!

Madi has a few creatures of her own here thanks to her dreams and for being a potential heir. She created Lord Brothwell one night and made him *exactly* like her and Amari. But now that Amari is the official heir to the throne, Hallam isn't going to accept Madi as an heir anymore.

Now, it's a race to get Madi back in Homba.

3

Amari grabs onto the ladder as Homba has an earthquake.

Fuck. This isn't good. Amari knows this. She knows everything about Hallam! Her grandfather told her stories about it and educated her on everything she needed to know about it! This better not be Kera's doing!

Or wait… Where's Madi? Amari is surprised Madi didn't crash the wedding! Adam didn't send Madi to Hallam, did he? Amari now knows what role Adam plays. He's a potential husband! A man that is considered to be the god of Hallam.

And Garrett! He's not just Amari's officiant. He's Nolan's creation! Nolan created some life that can cross between Homba and Hallam without throwing Hallam off.

Humans… It's the life that are complete myths that can't cross over! Not only do they knock Hallam off its core, but they just can't simply survive. Vampires that have lived for thousands of years would just wither away, leaving no trace of their existence behind. Homba is based on reality. Hallam is based on fiction. Myths and legends.

Amari waits the earthquake out, Mike holding onto her ankles. After a moment it dies down and everything goes back to normal. Amari is lucky this earthquake is no more than a 2.51 magnitude at best, barely shaking the things around her and Mike.

"Are you okay," Mike asks after everything calms down.

"Yeah," Amari replies.

"That was at least a two point five."

Amari looks down at Mike. "Add a one to that."

Mike pulls his head back at Amari. "When have you become an expert at earthquake magnitudes?"

"When you cheated on me three months prior."

Mike gives Amari his charming but cunning look, squinting his blue eyes with his lips in a thin line.

"Amari," he drawls out. "You know I wouldn't do that to you intentionally."

"Bull. Shit." Amari walks down the ladder and Mike gives her room, backing up and watching her. The fairy lights in hand Amari gets reminded of the earth fairy in Hallam.

Sunni is very light spirited and she has the fairy lights hung around in her home, which conveniently is the great oak in the middle of the forest Amari dreams about all the time. She really needs to pay Hallam a visit and take care of some business there.

Amari so wishes she could send Adam a mind link right now, but they're not in Hallam. A text will have to do. Amari pulls her phone out and pulls Adam's number up.

*Hey, are you close by?* Amari sends the text and she hears the back entry doors close. She notices her text to Adam getting read right away.

"How 'bout a I'm already here," Adam says as he walks into the gym.

Amari laughs at the convenience and she looks at her best friend.

"Does that work?"

"You know it does." Amari walks over to Adam and into his open arms. Even though he's a potential suitor for her back in Hallam, she doesn't think his wife would quite approve. "Hi."

"Hi." Adam rubs Amari's back. "Don't choose Klauss. His wife would *kill* him. And we both know she's very capable."

"Oh, I don't dream of it."

"You know who that leaves."

Amari looks up at Adam and his impeccable ocean blue eyes meet her brown eyes. Sometimes his eyes are green. "My officiant and his one rival."

Adam moans in agreement.

"Viggo," Amari and Adam say in unison.

"Who's Viggo," Mike asks from behind Amari.

Adam's blue eyes glare at him. "A blast from the past. Before you."

"That's impossible. I've been in Amari's whole entire life!" He's not wrong. Erika and Amari's mom are childhood best friends that never drifted apart no matter where their paths took them. They were always there for each other. And they helped each other when they both lost their husbands, who were best friends.

Amari pulls away from Adam's embrace and looks back at Mike.

"He's practically from another world." Amari puts her hands in her pockets and Adam snorts, stifling a laugh. It seems a lot of people have been having to stifle a laugh today!

Amari turns around to face Mike. She honestly doesn't know how else to describe the Viking that she has constantly dreamt about. He's smart, cunning, loyal… And very good looking. Take all of his armor and shirts off and you can just watch his muscles ripple as they work together from just a lift of his arm.

Amari loves that about Viggo. His embrace has always made her feel safe. He's a good pick indeed. But Garrett has a place in Amari's heart as well. This is going to be a good battle between the two good men.

They're very good friends. Amari recalls a dream of Viggo of when he told her a story about him and Garrett going head-to-head against a wild tafala together. Tafalas are basically a sea serpent. But they're much bigger, growing as long as fifty-two feet, and meaner. The tafala's have more of an oval shaped head, their jawlines lining up perfectly with the bottom of their round bodies.

"And he's best friends with your uncle," Amari finally says to Mike, breaking the silence. "Garrett."

Mike clenches his jaw, clearly not happy at the mention of his uncle that's literally just fifteen years older than him. His grandparents got married young, barely just turned seventeen and freshly graduated from high school. They had their oldest literally just two months after turning eighteen.

When they were thirty years-old they had Garrett, their last child. It doesn't help that Erika is twelve years older than him, being the oldest of all six siblings with Garrett as the only male. She was twenty-three when she married Mike's dad and twenty-seven when she had Mike. Eric came along when Mike was five years old. They would've had a sister between them. But she was a stillborn, the umbilical cord wrapped around her neck tightly.

Amari shrugs, watching Mike. "What?" She asks nonchalantly.

"You just had to mention my mom's brother," Mike says through his clenched teeth. "Not one of my dad's brothers."

Amari shrugs. "I never met any of their friends, now did I?"

Mike makes a sound in disgust. He turns away from Amari and Adam and starts wrapping all the fairy lights together, putting them in a tote as Amari turns and looks up at her beloved best friend.

"Is she," Amari starts lowly, not wanting Mike to hear.

"In Hallam," Adam finishes lowly for Amari. "Yeah. Your entitled cousin won't come back."

"Well, she has to."

"She thinks it's her world to control."

"And I will gladly step through and show her who the rightful heir is. I just have to finish this up with Mike."

"I know he's not his favorite person right now, but I contacted Garrett. He'll be here to take your place. You need to go and bring her back. Before she brings Hallam down into a crumble."

"What about…"

"Kera?"

Amari nods. "She can make it so that there's two rightful heirs to the throne at the same time."

"Jarom and Raja took care of her. She's in prison."

"To be honest I think that would be the perfect place for Madi to rule. Hell's Fire. It suits her quite nicely."

Adam opens his mouth to speak, but he stops himself, thinking on the matter. He closes his mouth after a moment as he starts to consider, his head tilted as he looks up at the ceiling. "Actually, that would work."

"Then make it happen."

Adam looks at Amari. "It's not that simple without you and Garrett there."

Amari sighs and sags, hanging her head. Adam holds a bag of food up. "I brought your thinking food."

"Dumplings," Amari breathes as she smells the food coming from the bag that's right in front of her. She watches it sway back and forth in Adam's hand, dangling from his fingers.

"With your favorite sauce."

"Wasabi mixed with teriyaki. Mmm," Amari growls in delight. "My favorite."

Adam drops the bag on Amari's hand and her fingers wrap around the plastic handles. "My wife's waiting for me at home. She didn't like it when I just got up and left."

Amari looks up at Adam after looking at her food in the bag. "Well, then why'd you leave for Ogden just for this?"

Adam shrugs. "I had a few errands to run in Ogden. I thought you'd like your favorite dumplings and rice."

"You know, Adam. Sometimes I could just kiss you."

Adam takes an inch closer to Amari, his nose almost brushing her nose teasingly. "I'm not on the market tonight," he teases, referring to their inside joke. Amari snorts and laughs, hanging her head and putting her palm on his chest.

When she and Adam went on a double date with his now wife and her now ex-boyfriend, who's over there putting fairy lights away, Amari told a man that hit on her with only Adam as her witness that she wasn't on the market that night and used Adam as her boyfriend, pulling him in to fully kiss him on the lips. They got a little too into it and pulled it off too neatly.

Amari smacked Adam in the face when they pulled away from each other and just stared into each other's eyes with his hand on her ass, telling him she wasn't on the market that night.

Amari lifts her head and looks up at Adam, his ocean blue eyes meeting her brown eyes. They both hold back a smirk.

"Hallam," Adam says softly after a quiet moment.

"Yeah," Amari drawls out. "Yep."

∞

Madi's back meets the wall as her lips fuse with Ryker's.

They take a deep breath through their noses and he slides her up the wall, getting in between her thighs. Oh, she hates that the man she created can't be hers. The people are trying to force her back into Homba, but she doesn't want to go. She wants to stay here. With her lover she's dreamt about in the past.

Madi has a flashback to a dream where she and Ryker made passionate love. His hands caressed her naked skin, his shaft penetrated her opening, stroking her insides and making her climax. Madi remembers the love making that happened almost every night with this man and she wants a night with him. She wants eternity with him!

Ryker rips open Madi's blouse and his hand massages her naked breast. Oh, yes. She wants this. Madi unbuckles Ryker's belt and he gladly pushes his pants and boxers down.

"You're in deep trouble for this," Ryker breathes, looking at Madi's lips.

She wraps her arms around his neck and her brown eyes meet with his green eyes. "Then punish me," she whispers seductively.

Ryker rips Madi's leggings with one swift move and they expose her black lace panties. Their lips meet as he sticks two fingers inside of her as the head of his cock barely presses into her clitoris, her panties pushed to the side.

Pleasure sweeps over her and she gets blinded by it. Madi tries to fight it, but Ryker always knows her weakness. Her eyes roll to the back of her head and she lays her head back against the wall. Ryker's lips land on Madi's neck and he guides himself inside of her. Dear god… He's going to be the death of her. Madi can never resist Ryker!

He thrusts into her then lets himself pull out until the tip of his shaft is barely pressing into her. He thrusts into her, again, going all the way inside of her to the hilt. Then he pulls out of her with the tip of his shaft barely pressing into her. He continues to thrust into her this way, taking her to her climax.

Ryker marks Madi's neck, leaving a hickie at the base of it on the side. Oh, she can't get enough of him! Ryker picks up the speed until he can't hold back anymore. Madi makes a small sound in pleasure.

"Oh, Daddy," Madi moans. She throws her shoulders back and presses her naked breasts into Ryker's chest.

He holds onto her thighs and rails her, his thrusts even harder and faster. Madi's nails dig into Ryker's arms as she orgasms and he thrusts into her one last time. As she comes back to him, they pant in unison. His lips brush against her lips. He rests his forehead on her forehead as they close their eyes, enjoying the moment.

But it doesn't last long. A man clears his throat from behind Ryker.

"It's time to go, sir," Lamar, Ryker's butler, says. "You don't want to be late."

Ryker growls a grunt and clears his throat, lifting his head and looking up at the ceiling. "Right... Just give us another moment."

"You're already pushing it, Lord Brothwell."

Ryker growls in disappointment. He looks at Madi. "I'll be back within the hour. I got something to take care of."

"Is it something I can help with?" Madi hears a small sound that tingles the hair on her neck.

"No." Ryker clears his throat. "But if you want to come greet your cousin with me, you can. She and I have business to attend to."

Something snaps inside of Madi and anger replaces the love she was just feeling in her chest. "Why the fuck is she in charge?"

"Because she's been officiated as the rightful heir to Hallam. She will be crowned as our goddess."
Madi snorts in disgust. "That should be me."

"We'll be talking about you, too. But you need clothes on that aren't ripped. And I can't wait up for you."

Madi looks away in disappointment. "Fine," she says lowly.

Ryker kisses Madi's jaw. "I love you." He lingers his lips on her skin as he surprises Madi with his words. "I won't be too long."

Madi nods her head, looking down. Ryker pulls away and lets her slide back down the wall. Madi's feet meet the floor and she rearranges herself the best she can. She covers her naked breasts with her shirt and uses her power to fix it since it's fixable. Her pants not so much.

"I'll see you in a while." Ryker kisses Madi's temple and she nods her head, looking up at him.

"I'll come join you in a bit," she replies, not wanting Amari to make any decisions without her there.

They may not like each other and Madi has disowned Amari. But Madi was once a potential heir to the throne and now she gets nothing for creating a little bit of the life here. She deserves something!

Ryker nods his head and he walks out of the room. Madi looks at Lamar, who keeps his eyes on her face while her shirt gets fixed with the little bit of magic she has left.

"You may not have a place here anymore," Lamar starts to say. He shakes his head at Madi. "But don't go looking for Kera to make a place here. She's bad news."

"What did she do?" Interested in finding out more about this world, Madi wants to know everything. She could use the information to get what she wants!

"Cast a lot of spells on Hallam to make it unstable. Amelia, her oldest, was able to get rid of most of them with the help of her sister."

"Alia."

Lamar nods his head. "Yes. Amelia wanted to get rid of all of the spells and we were blinded from the truth." Lamar shakes his head. "We thought Amelia was the bad one. There was a great war over it."

"What happened?"

"Amari saved the day. In her dream, of course. But she had her partner in crime with her and they were able to take the creatures down and find out the truth. Amari wanted to kill Kera, but Raja had different plans."

Madi nods her head, curious to know more. "So, she's trapped."

Lamar nods his head in agreement. "In Hell's Fire. Hellhounds and wyverns guard it."

That sounds like something that needs a person to look over! Why isn't there someone like Hades taking care of it? Madi's time here in Hallam has taught her a lot even though she's only been here for a day. She wants to be the goddess of Hallam and make sure Hell's Fire stays protected and watched over at all times!

Madi doesn't want Hallam to be unstable! Madi shakes her head as she remembers something that Lamar said. She looks at him through narrowed eyes.

"Wait… You said that Amelia and Alia took care of *most*. Of the spells. Is there still a few cast on Hallam?"

Lamar nods his head. "One. Amelia just got rid of a few. And the spell can only be removed with Amari here to look over it."

"And what spell is that?"

"The binding spell. It keeps the myths bound here. They can never cross over because of it."

Madi nods her head, getting an idea. She's intrigued. She knows how to become the goddess of Hallam!

4

Amari twists her wrist, her hand in a fist, as she starts across the street and towards Manning's Short Stop.

Here at this location, she'll be able to open the portal to her backyard. The road turns into blocks and does the wave as Amari walks across and lifts her other hand up, her palm facing up. She holds the position with her hands as the portal opens near the gas station, her fist next to her side and her palm up in the air above her head with her arm extended.

Amari steps through the portal then closes it behind her, opening her fist to stretch her hand out wide and letting her other hand fall down with the palm facing down. Booties, a cat she had until having to put him down two and a half years ago, jumps into her arms to greet her into Hallam.

Amari instantly stops and wraps her arms around him, burying her face into his fur. She completely forgot! Her grandpa told her stories about Hallam and one of

those was seeing her dog Rascal here in Hallam after
Rascal passed back in Homba!

Before any being goes to heaven after they pass,
they have the opportunity to choose a life here in Hallam
to live as long as they did back in Homba. It's like a
second chance at life.

"Oh, Booties," Amari moans into Booties' fur.
"I've missed you."

Booties meows and he sounds exactly like Amari
remembers. She tightens her hold on him.

"Me too, love. Me too."

A dog whines next to Amari, his whine way too
familiar.

"Sodes," Amari exclaims. She bends down to the
eye level of her dog that's half black lab and half
malamute. "It's so good to see you!"

Amari hugs Lasodo's neck, his long fur showing
his age. His body is black with the tips a light brown
underneath his belly. His tail is in a similar manner. His
muzzle is white and gets whiter with age, the tips of the
black around his eyes turning gray. His legs are a light
brown with the long tips white and his paws are white.

Lasodo has floppy ears and it's his bright blue
eyes that show he's a mut with malamute blood. His left
eye has a small brown triangle pointing to his pupil from
the top of the iris.

Lasodo starts to growl in Amari's ear and she knows something is up. She looks up from his neck and spots three pairs of red eyes glowing in the dark not too far from her gardens.

Hellhounds. Booties gets on Amari's shoulders as she stands up and hisses at the three hellhounds that are watching. Their eyes land on Booties and they back up, knowing damn well what a cat can do to a hellhound.

Cats are usually pretty good at keeping hellhounds in Hell. Maybe it's time for Amari to create more cats to keep them in Hell's Fire here in Hallam. Madi can help with that as well.

Amari quietly summons her light swords and they slide down her arms and into her hands. Lasodo stands in front of Amari, growling at the hellhounds with his fur bristled and standing on end. Where it's just three hellhounds it will be a piece of cake for just Booties to handle them. But if there's more waiting in the forest, Booties is going to need all the help he can get.

A long-haired tuxedo cat, his fur standing on end makes him look twice his size. And if he were to shift into his Guardian form, his fur would actually turn into bristles. Amari looks around for clues for more hellhounds nearby. But nothing.

"Trouble sleeping," a familiar male voice asks teasingly.

"Henry," Amari says. She glances at her butler then back at the hellhounds, who are no longer there. But Booties and Lasodo don't let their hair down.

Booties growls, ready to take on the hellhounds. Amari stands as normal and looks at Henry.

"So glad to see you."

"Yes!"

Amari starts for Henry and they meet in the middle of her gardens, hugging each other. Amari wraps her arms around Henry's torso and his arms go around her shoulder.

"It's so good to finally have you here. We've been worried sick since you haven't dreamt about Hallam for a couple weeks, now."

"Adult life." Amari sets her chin on Henry's shoulder, standing a few inches shorter than him. "You tend to get super busy and not have any dreams when you sleep."

"You need a melatonin."

Amari laughs. Henry pulls back and looks at Amari, holding onto her shoulders. His green eyes meet her brown eyes in a soft and excited expression.

"Welcome home," Henry says softly.

"Thank you."

"Congratulations are in order."

"Yes! Thank you! I'm excited."

"And uh…" Henry trails off as he gets a teasing look in his eyes. "You're shorter than I remember." He teases.

"So, are you," Amari teases.

Henry laughs. "Come." He wraps his arm around Amari and walks beside her towards the estate. "Lord Brothwell will be here soon to talk."

"Can I have a moment to talk to my most favorite butler in the world?" Amari looks up at her beloved butler as he leads her into her estate.

He laughs full-heartedly, his laugh soft and somehow filling the night sky. "Yes, of course."

"How's your family?"

"Good! My wife is now cancer free and our youngest just had her first child."

"Congratulations!"

"Thank you. She had a tough pregnancy, but we're glad the baby is healthy. No diabetes."

Amari tilts her head. "Gestational?"

"Yes. Anya had to have some of the strangest breakfasts."

"So, did my sister. She had it with her second child."

"Well." Henry leads Amari to her office, walking around the extravagant staircase and turning left into the spacious room. "I will go get tea for you and Lord Brothwell. Unless…"

Amari slips out of Henry's warm embrace and turns to look back at him. "Will you send Ada in, please? She's part witch and has some of the most unique techniques to keep you awake."

"Yes, of course."

"Thank you, Henry. I appreciate it."

"You are most definitely welcome." Henry leaves Amari in her office and she walks over to her desk. She sits down in her comfortable rolling chair that has back support and grabs the top file from a stack in her divider. Amari opens it and goes over the paperwork. She sighs and sags in disappointment to find out the file has Allah's name all over it.

He wants to expand… Again. This is the fifth time, Allah! What the fuck is going on?! The door to Amari's office opens and closes quietly.

"Queen Amari," Ada's familiar small voice says softly. "I mean… Goddess Amari. It's so good to finally have you here."

Amari puts the file down with a sigh and rubs her forehead, her eyes closed. "Thank you, Ada. It's nice to finally be here in person. I just wish your king would stop trying to expand."

"He just wants the good for the world."

"Yeah, well. He's tiresome."

Ada gets behind Amari and pushes the button on the armrest of Amari's chair to lower the back rest for better access to her head and neck. "Let me fix that," Ada seduces softly.

Amari leans her head back into Ada's hands as Ada massages it. "You're my favorite wolf. You know that, right?"

"Only because I'm lesbian." Ada digs her elbows into Amari's shoulders as she deepens her massage on Amari's head.

Amari moans, her eyes closed. "That's not the only reason."

Ada puts her lips to Amari's ear. "You wanna take this to the bedroom?"

"Wake me up first," Amari says low. "And then once my meeting with Lord Brothwell is over, I'll meet you in your bedroom."

"Not yours, your majesty?" Ada coos.

"I prefer to do it where my maids are most comfortable."

Ada moans in Amari's ear as she massages Amari's shoulder. "As you wish, my goddess," Ada whispers seductively. Her mouth goes on Amari's neck and she pulls the skin into her mouth.

Amari moans a small release of pleasure. "Give me a hickie and I'll have to discipline you."

Ada doesn't respond. Nor does she stop. She continues to suck on Amari's neck and pleasure Amari with her mouth. Ada pulls her mouth away after a moment, making popping sound from sucking. Her lips instantly go to Amari's lips.

"Then discipline me," Ada seduces in a whisper. "Cause I've been a bad, bad girl, your majesty." Ada trails her thumbs up the back of Amari's neck then braces Amari's head in her hands.

Ada cracks Amari's neck then wraps her right arm around Amari's head. She braces her left arm into Amari's head and cracks Amari's head and neck that way. Then she switches positions with her arms and cracks Amari's head and neck the other direction.

Amari moans at the release from all the tension and Ada bends her head down.

"You're an angel," Amari says lowly, unsure if Ada caught her words.

Ada wakes Amari up with another crack in the neck, pulling her head up. Then she massages Amari's temples. Amari goes quiet as a wave of energy bursts through her body from Ada's touch.

Then Ada disappears all of a sudden, leaving Amari in a state of relaxation. Amari opens her eyes and pushes the button for her back rest to come back up. She leans into it as a few knocks sound on her door and Lord Brothwell peeks in.

"I have an order for one Miss Amari Greenwood," Lord Brothwell says, his deep blue eyes focused on Amari. They were probably green just a moment ago, though. Amari's estate has the brightest lights that bring out the real color of your eyes.

"What kind of order?" Amari watches him, her fingertips pressed into each other with her elbows on her armrests.

"A quarter pounder with cheese, extra pickles and onion, a large jamocha shake, and a large fry."

Amari snorts and smiles. "How do you know me when Madi is your creator?"

Lord Brothwell tilts his head in a shrug. "That's what she told me you like."

"That's what I had when I was fat. I would get the quarter pounder and fries from McDonalds and of course you can only get a jamocha shake at Arby's."

"Well, I got them specially ordered for you," Lord Brothwell teases.

"Get in here, handsome."

"Oh, good." He whispers as he comes inside. He closes the door quietly behind him. He tiptoes over to Amari with two bags of food and a drink carton with two jamocha shakes.

One bag is from McDonalds and the other is from Arby's. "You weren't kidding."

Lord Brothwell sets the drink carton down on Amari's desk then sits in one of the chairs in front of it. He sets the bags on her desk as he sits down. Then he looks over at her.

"Don't worry," Lord Brothwell starts softly. "I got the burgers in lettuce wraps and I got the curly fries instead of McDonald's fries."

"No kidding," Amari draws out. She leans over and grabs the Arby's bag. "I don't even remember having a McDonald's and Arby's here."

"Madi literally had a dream about them being in the mall just the other night. They got all of the regular stuff and menus from the ones back in Homba."

"Thank you, Madi." Amari eats a curly fry out of the Arby's bag. She looks at Lord Brothwell. "You know, I feel bad Garrett just officiated me as the rightful heir to the throne. Madi deserves half of it since we both created life here."

"You're right. And she *really* wants to be the goddess."

The idea hits Amari, again, and she looks up. If she were a cartoon, a light bulb would be over her head. "What about Hell's Fire?"

Lord Brothwell looks up at Amari after pulling his sandwich out of the McDonald's bag. He reaches over and takes the Arby's bag from Amari, his blue eyes on her brown eyes. "I think she would like that."

"She'd be able to create her own life." Amari goes through her files in her divider, looking for the right one.

"With. Limits."

"She'd be able to keep the hellhounds in check. They're getting out of control."

"I literally just watched Booties chase a few off in Guardian form before I walked in. An orange Guardian was beside him."

Amari nods her head. "Jake. I remember seeing a video about his passing back in Homba."

"Well." Lord Brothwell pulls the one large container of curly fries out of the Arby's and lays it on some napkins on Amari's desk. "Let's talk about Madi's new role here."

Amari smirks at Lord Brothwell as she finds the right file. A couple hours go by as they talk about and plan Madi's officiation and crowning as Hell's Fire's goddess.

They go over everything and agree on a day and time. It will happen after Amari's crowning. After two hours go by, they wrap things up and Amari follows Lord Brothwell over to the door.

He opens it and stands in the doorway, looking at Amari.

"Thank you," he says softly, appreciation in his eyes. "I really appreciate it."

"Hey," Amari says softly. She takes a step closer to Lord Brothwell. "I know you do. But just don't get attached to her."

Lord Brothwell searches Amari's eyes. "Why?"

"She has a boyfriend back in Homba."

Lord Brothwell's heart starts to break.

"I'm so sorry. I thought she would've told you."

He shakes his head. "No. She never said a word."

"Nothing?"

Lord Brothwell shakes his head again. "Before I came. We actually…"

Amari knows exactly where Lord Brothwell is going and her heart breaks for him. She pulls him into a hug and his arms wrap around her torso, his chin on her shoulder.

"I'm so sorry," she says softly. "Madi does this. She did it to Mike and I, making Mike cheat on me with her. Then a week later she turned around and had sex with his brother. Madi and Eric have been inseparable ever since."

Lord Brothwell shudders as he exhales, his breath sounding ragged. Amari rubs his back, her arms wrapped around his shoulders.

"I'm so sorry," she whispers in his ear.

"Well… After her crowning I won't have to deal with her. That's for sure."

"Yeah," Amari draws out softly, trying to soothe Lord Brothwell. She rubs his back. She sets her hand on the top of his head and puts her lips to his ear. "She can stay here when she comes back for her crowning."

"That'd be great," Lord Brothwell says softly.

"Kay." Amari rubs Lord Brothwell's back soothingly one last time then she lets him go.

He pulls back and looks at her gratefully. He grabs her elbow. "Thank you, Amari."

"You're welcome, Lord Brothwell."

"Please. Call me Ryker."

"Okay… Ryker."

Lord Brothwell squeezes Amari's elbow then starts for the front door. Madi decides to make an entrance, wearing high-waisted skinny jeans with holes all over the legs, leaving very little to the imagination of her good-looking legs and a beige crop top that's off the shoulders.

Madi looks at Amari and their brown eyes meet. Madi glances at Ryker then her brown eyes are back on Amari's, knowing exactly what went down.

"Ryker," Madi starts.

"Don't." Ryker stops Madi. "You're going to have part of Hallam. Hell's Fire will be your world to rule over. Don't worry. It's not as bad as it sounds."

Madi watches Ryker with a broken heart as he opens the door and walks out. She looks at Amari after a moment with a glare. "Did you honestly have to tell him?"

Amari holds her chin up high, keeping eye contact with her cousin. "I honestly wish I didn't have to. But he had no idea."

"I would've told him."

"Maybe when you got stuck here."

"When will that be? Cause I honestly would like to be able to say goodbye to my friends and family. Queen Amari," Madi spats.

"A couple weeks."

Madi nods.

"You're staying in the east wing tonight. If you haven't eaten, one of the cooks can warm up a bowl of soup for you."

"I'm good."

"Kay. You're going back to Homba early in the morning. I'll let you through the portal that takes you to Corinne."

"No buses go through there."

"Don't worry. Your boyfriend will be waiting for you." Amari turns and starts for the maids' quarters, leaving Madi to her own accords.

Amari passes the kitchen, in the hallway, then turns left into the living room of the maids' quarters. She finds her way to Ada's bedroom and quietly slips in.

"Amari," Ada calls softly. "Is that you?"

Amari quickly walks over to Ada and stops her from getting out of bed, shushing her and getting in her face. Amari tucks the covers aside a little as she straddles Ada and kisses her. "Don't get out of bed. Don't move."

"Oh," Ada moans seductively. Her blue-green eyes shine bright in the starlight that shines through her open window.

"You took care of me earlier. Now, it's my turn."

"Yes, Momma. I want you to take care of me."

Amari tears Ada's nighty in two and looks at her luscious round breasts. "Mine," Amari growls. She leans in and takes Ada's breast in her mouth, sucking the nipple in and flicking it with her tongue.

Ada gasps and grasps onto Amari's hair, trapping her head against Ada's breast. Amari lays Ada back down on her bed and gives her breast a hickie, marking her.

Ada's pants fill the room as Amari continues to make out with her breast. Her hand lands next to Ada's head. Good, lord! If Ada gets Amari going just with her breasts, Amari's not going to be able to stop herself! Ada unbuckles Amari's belt and unzips her pants. She's able to pop the button off Amari's pants with one swift move and she slips her hand into Amari's wetness, stroking Amari's opening, lips, and clitoris.

Amari growls into Ada's breast and sends the vibrations throughout her body. Ada gasps and pants, getting Amari going. Amari trails her lips up Ada's chest and they land on her mate mark. Amari licks it and makes out with it, wishing her own mark is there. But she can't claim her maids, manservants, butler, and housekeeper just yet. She has to wait until after her crowning.

As Ada fucks Amari's opening with two fingers inside of her Amari sucks on Ada's mate mark and fucks her opening with two fingers. Ada groans in pleasure and throws her head back, pressing her breasts into Amari's breasts.

Amari knows she's done it before, but does she dare let her clitoris grow? Or should she play it safe and use a strap-on?

"Use it," Ada whispers in Amari's ear.

Amari moans into Ada's neck. "Strap-on," she says into Ada's neck, making it an order.

"I wanna feel you instead."

"Are you sure? I can only do it once a year."

"Use it," Ada seduces, wrapping her free arm around Amari's shoulder while she continues to fuck Amari's opening with her other hand. "And I'll use mine."

Amari quickly gets rid of all of her clothes and Ada watches her, rubbing her own clitoris and preparing it for what's about to come. Amari straddles Ada, her naked backside on Ada's pelvis. If they're both going to do it, they gotta do it like this.

Ada has the rare gene to grow her clitoris into a penis all thanks to Amari's dreams, where she did it multiple times. Sad thing is they can't do this very often. Their clitoris has to heal from the stretch. Amari closes her eyes and focuses on her clitoris, feeling it out and rubbing it with her finger to give it stimulation. She closes her eyes in a flutter as pleasure hits her.

After a minute Amari focuses and her clitoris grows into a ten-inch penis. She feels Ada's pressing into her backside. Amari lifts herself up then lowers her opening on Ada's penis as she sinks her penis into Ada's opening. The pleasure hits Amari right away and she falls onto her hands, grabbing onto Ada's shins. Ada grabs onto Amari's hips and thrusts into her opening, stroking her insides and making her penis feel the tightness envelope around it. The pleasure is too much.

Amari thrusts into Ada as Ada thrusts into her and their pelvises smack hard. Amari gapes as she has an orgasm and she keeps thrusting into Ada. They get into a rhythm, pulling their hips back at the same time and smacking into each other. In sync, they have orgasm after orgasm, unable to stop themselves from thrusting into each other even harder and panting with pleasure uncontrollably.

Amari can feel her orgasm heighten and her knuckles turn white from her tight grip around Ada's shins, her penis feeling Ada's tightness as Ada's penis strokes her insides. Fuck! No wonder their clitorises need time to heal from this! It's pure bliss!

Amari's eyes roll to the back of her head as she and Ada continue their thrusts into each other, feeling each other's tightness around their penises while their openings also get pleasured. Blinded by pleasure, Amari lifts her head as she groans, her groan staccato from the thrusts.

Amari's breasts bounce violently, hanging free. She hears Ada behind her, Ada's voice high-pitched from the pleasure. Ada voices her pants as
the pace picks up.

"Oh, yeah," Ada breathes. "Goddess. Amari!"

Amari growls at the sound of Ada saying her
name.

"Amari, momma! Fuck me! I'm yours!" Ada growls, unable to control herself.

Amari has another orgasm at Ada's sounds of pleasure and she thrusts into Ada so hard Ada screams her name, waking up all the maids and manservants. Amari stays deep inside of Ada as her wetness spreads into Ada, pleasure taking over and spreading throughout her whole entire body. Fuck!

"Ada," Amari screams a growl. "Fuck, you're perfect!" Amari thrusts into Ada even harder and shoots her wetness inside of her, again, unable to control herself. She has an orgasm, again.

Ada's wetness shoots inside of Amari and they swap a couple eggs. This is why only women get the rare gene. Usually, lesbians get the rare gene so they can shoot a couple of their eggs into another woman, who is willing to have sex with a man and give the lesbian a child. That is why a lesbian usually pairs up with a bisexual woman. This way they can have a child with their male mate if they have one with no guilt.

There's a werecat clan and a werewolf pack that both have a trio that does this. It works out in the end. Amari yells in pleasure and throws her head back, unable to get enough. She's going to be doing it with Ada all night!

Ada thrusts into Amari hard and the headboard smacks against the wall over and over again. Fuck! Yes! Oh, yes! Again. Ada's and Amari's pelvises smack in unison, making the loudest smack that echoes in the bedroom. Amari crumbles on top of Ada as she climaxes and shakes from the biggest orgasm that a woman could ever have.

They booth shoot another pair of eggs inside of each other. Ada grabs Amari's thighs, pulling her back slightly, then rolls on top of her, railing Amari into the bed until she feels like all of the eggs she contains inside of her are no longer just her own.

"Take them," Ada growls a scream. "Take every single one of them!"

Amari's eyes roll to the back of her head as her penis stays deep inside of Ada as she takes dominance and rails Amari into the bed, Amari's opening screaming for a release that only involves a bigger pounding. And a much bigger penis.

"Give him my kids," Ada growls in frustration, digging her fingers into Amari's thighs. "And then some," she growls as she thrusts even harder with every thrust. Ada pulls Amari's penis out of her opening, but the pleasure doesn't stop. It just intensifies. Amari gasps at the sudden spots that she sees at the back of her head.

How is this possible?

"I don't want any of my eggs," Ada growls as she continues to spill ever single egg of hers into Amari and gives all of Amari's back. "I don't ever wanna warm his bed! Take it!" Ada thrusts into Amari even harder, making Amari bounce on the bed with her breasts springing up and smacking her in the face. "And take him, too!" Ada's furious, never wanting a man to touch her ever, again. "Take this, Allah. And this!"

Ada keeps thrusting into Amari and spilling every single one of her seeds into Amari, hitting Amari's spot every single time and driving her to her ecstasy. Ada doesn't stop until her ovaries are screaming at her, telling her that she has no more eggs to give.

And Amari's eggs are back inside of her. Ada collapses onto her bed, in between Amari's legs, and pants as she shakes, having the biggest and most intimate orgasm ever with Amari. They pant in unison, their eyes rolled to the back of their heads. Good, lord! Amari's going to turn lesbian after this! Ada cries into her pillow, her penis still deep inside of Amari. But Amari's penis shrinks back into her inch by inch until it's formed back into a clitoris.

Fuck! Amari has all of her eggs back and now all of Ada's eggs as well!

# 5

Viggo casts his fishing net into the ocean and secures the ends on his ship. He's determined to keep his catch today. He won't let the wild tafalas get this catch! There might be twenty of them. But Viggo has figured out that if he sets sail very early in the morning, he'll be able to catch some fish with no problem. But he also brought his teenaged dragon with him this time. Brom might be able to fight off the tafalas.

Tafalas are meaner and wilder when they don't have a rider. Luckily, that doesn't happen very often. A lot of them like the company of a rider. But once in a while a tafala will choose to go rider free once they hit the age to choose.

Viggo walks over to the main mast and loosens the rope. Once it all falls down to the floor, he unrolls it and tosses it behind him. Viggo wraps up the rope in his hands and sets it down nicely. The main sail is trying to come loose and catch wind. He can't afford to move.

This is the spot for good fish like salmon, salt water trout, and cod.

Viggo rolls the sail in tighter then starts to tighten his rope. Once he's reassured about the sail being tightly rolled, he secures his rope, tightening it until it can't be tightened anymore and using the sailor's knot to secure it. There. That should hold it.

Viggo hears a low rumbling sound close by. Fuck. This isn't good. He quickly runs over to the side and shines a light on the water. But he doesn't see anything. He hears the low rumble again and the sun starts peaking over the mountains just a tad. The sun gets blocked by something and Viggo hears water dripping. Some of the drips hit the water, but some also hit the foredeck.

Viggo looks up at the tafala that's towering over his ship, the massive sea snake looking right at him. He drops his flashlight, shocked at how big he has grown. The tafala's head looks similar to an electric eel's head, but it looks more muscular and oval shaped with box ends for the jaw.

Tafala males usually weigh as much as a tyrannosaurus rex at the length of fifty-two feet. The females usually weigh about eight tons and grow to be fifty feet long. But this one… He's much bigger. And it's why he's the king.

"Ambroz," Viggo finally says after recovering from his shock. He holds his hand out to the tafala. "Old friend. You've grown!" He couldn't believe his eyes! If only Amari were here to see him!

Ambroz lowers his head towards Viggo and rests his nose into the palm of Viggo's hand. He's huge! He's probably what? Twenty tons and sixty feet long? That's just as big as a Spinosaurus!

"I've missed you."

"I missed you, too," Ambroz says to Viggo, his deep voice echoing in Viggo's mind.

"You've been busy, I see."

"Yes. Lots of water to cover and many clans to visit. You're lucky I found you on a good start for the morning."

Viggo smirks at his friend. "Can you do me a favor before you leave?"

"Anything."

"Please teach the wild tafalas a lesson. They keep taking my catch."

"Let's see what I can do." Ambroz sends out a massive wave in a low frequency, rocking Viggo's ship.

Brom growls from behind Viggo. But Viggo is able to make him back down and be quiet with just a motion of his hand, keeping his eyes on his beloved friend. He wants to watch this. A call is heard in the distance and Viggo knows he's now safe.

"I'll see you next year," Ambroz says.

"See you then, brother," Viggo replies. He watches Ambroz dive into the water and swim away, letting his head and body go in and out of the surface of the ocean.

Viggo walks over to his net and he starts to pull it in. The net extra heavy, Viggo asks for help from Brom. Together they pull the net in to discover a juvenile great white shark made it into the net somehow. Brom dips his head and gently pushes the shark out of the net. Then he helps Viggo bring in his big catch of salmon, cod, and yes. Even a few halibut. That's odd! Viggo usually catches the halibut on a line!

Viggo quickly gets the fish in the port with the sturgeon he caught on a line earlier. Then he readies his sails. He would start the motor, but there's no reason to fix the propeller that a wild tafala smashed just the other day. Wind catches the sails as they fall down after their ropes are loosened.

Viggo walks over to the wheel and keeps it steady as the wind sails him across the ocean. An hour and a half later, he's setting his feet on a dock and securing his ship to it. Viggo sets shop up then starts gutting all of the fish.

The line of shoppers grows until they're finally let through. Viggo sells quite a bit of fish by the time busy hours are over. When they're over he has two sturgeon, one halibut, fifteen salmon, eight cod, and ten saltwater trout left.

"Hey, Viggo," a low familiar male voice says.

"Kim," Viggo exclaims, looking at his fellow deep-sea fisher. "Great to see you!" He walks over and hugs the man. They slap each other's backs then take a step back from each other. "How's the family?"

"Great! My wife is pregnant. Again."

Viggo laughs. "You can't keep her off you, can you?"

"Ah," Kim drawls out. "What can I say? Eight kids and still counting."

"Don't you wanna be done?"

"Oh, most definitely. But I can't convince the wife to get a hysterectomy. Or let me get a vasectomy." Kim says lowly, his head dipped low.

"You'll just have to do it in secret." Viggo replies lowly.

"Oh. Pffft! Anna is like the C-I-A around here. They could hire her back in Homba if she ever applied!"

"Well, good luck, then."

"Thank you." Kim looks at Viggo's fish. "Think we can do a trade?"

"Of course!" Viggo walks over to the biggest sturgeon he has, which is hanging on a hook.

"Think I can take the halibut this time? My wife's been craving it."

"Cravings never cease. Good luck!" Viggo walks over to the eight-foot, five-hundred-pound halibut and takes it down with Kim's help. They lay it down on his cart of goods.

"Do I have something good to trade for it."

"Oh, I would love to see what you have."

"Swordfish." Kim throws back a blanket in his cart to reveal a nine-foot swordfish. "One of my friends caught it on my ship when we went fishing yesterday. It's already gutted."

Viggo looks at Kim. "It's always a pleasure doing business with you, Kim." He lends his hand to Kim and they shake hands.

"Let me help you pack up."

"Thank you. I'd appreciate the help."

∞

Amari thrusts into Ada so hard that both of their breasts bounce against each other, the strap-on attached to Amari with an eight-inch dildo inside of her and a twelve-inch dildo inside of Ada.

Good, lord! It was bad enough Amari woke up horny after the most intense and intimate sex last night! She had to get Madi back in Homba and do some paperwork right away, leaving Ada asleep in bed. Amari saw Madi off, creating the portal that's in her gardens. She turned to Madi before Madi stepped through.

"I'll deliver the papers for your crowning when it gets closer to the date," Amari said to Madi.

Madi nodded her head then stepped through after making sure no one was around in Homba to see.

After doing some paperwork and having lunch with her maids and manservants like she sometimes does, Amari couldn't take it anymore. Watching Ada as she played with her hair and kept giving Amari looks, licking her lips just for Amari whenever she caught her eye, Amari had the hardest time keeping it casual. She got so horny by just watching Ada's lips meet her spoon.

It wasn't until after their small lunch Amari pulled Ada away before she could help clean up and brought her back to her bedroom. Now, Amari has Ada in her arms, their naked breasts pressed together, their fingers curled around each other's shoulders, their legs wrapped around each other, and their pelvises clashing into each other.

Their sweat mingles together as Amari continues to dominate Ada after Ada's episode last night. Amari is only an inch taller than Ada, making their sexual intercourses more intimate with their breaths mingling together. Ada is so Amari's mistress and girlfriend while she marries Garrett. He's always been supportive of her.

While Amari was nailing a woman she met at a mid-singles activity for their LDS religion, Garrett was patiently waiting for her in the next room over. He never admitted it to her, but she did hear him admitting to Viggo in a dream one of those nights that it turns him on to hear two women going at it. Amari thrusts the dildo deeply into Ada and Ada chokes on a moan, her mouth wide open and her head thrown back. Amari puts her mouth to Ada's mate mark and lets her breath caress it.

"Ada," Amari says lowly, her voice filled with lust. "Gosh. Ada!" The eight-inch dildo inside her strokes her and hits her spot multiple times, making her orgasm and see white.

Ada squeals in pleasure and her nails dig into Amari's shoulders. It turns Amari on more and she picks up the pace, thrusting into harder and at a much faster speed. Amari's pelvis smacks against Ada's pelvis very loudly and the headboard hits the wall.

"Fuck!" Amari yells as she orgasms. Her eyes roll to the back of her head and she clenches onto Ada for dear life.

"Amari," Ada screams. "Uh," she gasps loudly, throwing her head back as her eyes roll to the back of her head.

Amari and Ada orgasm together and Amari finally thrusts into Ada one last time, thrusting into her so hard the headboard knocks the picture above them off the wall. Their breaths mingle together as they cling onto each other and shake from their orgasms.

It takes Amari a moment, but she finally comes back down from her cloud and she watches Ada take longer to come back. Once she does, her eyes roll back to the front of her head and she looks up at the woman that she claims as her own. Her chosen mate if she could just get rid of her fated mate. Amari smiles and laughs, the vibrations going through Ada's body and pleasuring her.

"You're so gorgeous when you orgasm," Amari compliments Ada. She pulls the dildo out of Ada and takes the strap-on off, setting it aside on the night stand.

Ada gets up on her elbows and watches Amari. "So are you, my goddess," she flirts.

Amari looks at Ada as she sets the strap-on aside, putting it back in the drawer of Ada's nightstand. "You can't flirt with me without consequences, little missy."

"What consequences?"

"The kind that get you disciplined." Amari leans over Ada with her lips just inches away from Ada's, her hands on either side of Ada's hips.

Ada tosses her beach blond hair back and lets her blue-green eyes pierce Amari's brown eyes innocently. "Oh, but my lady! You can't discipline me in public! That would be… Inhumane! Animalistic!"

"Smacking of the ass and groping it," Amari flirts with Ada, a smile on her face. She lets her eyes soften Ada's with just a look, her lips just an inch away this time. "You should try it sometime."

Ada's eyes land on Amari's lips and Amari's eyes does the same. Amari closes in the gap and her lips clash with Ada's lips. She doesn't let up and lays Ada back down, her arm around Ada's waist.

"I so wanna mark you already," Amari says against Ada's lips. "Claim you. Dominate you in bed. And make sure you never leave. Do you understand?"

Ada giggles into Amari's lips and wraps her arm around Amari's shoulder.

"Oh, I understand," a familiar low and husky male voice from Amari's dreams says. "And it's not gonna happen," he threatens. "Cause Ada's my *fated mate*."

Amari instantly throws herself off of Ada and falls off the bed, staring at Allah. Fuck. Him? It could've been anyone but him! The lycan king and god of the were-kind. Fuck! He's going to *kill* Amari! She looks up at Ada, who is covering herself up and staying on the bed.

"Ada," Amari says. "Baby."

"Hmm?" Ada looks down at Amari.

"When were you going to tell me?"

"Now." Ada looks frightened. And she has every right to be. She's mated to the most powerful man in Hallam! Ada looks at Allah.

"Ada, please go draw yourself a bath and relax. Your mate and I need to talk."

"Oh, we're going to do more than talk," Allah growls threateningly.

Amari looks up at him just to meet his death glare. But what else is in that look? Lust? That can't be right! She's gotta be dreaming! Allah doesn't like her that way!

Well... There was that one dream almost a whole year ago...

6

Lillian throws a kick at a man's head before she catches a throwing fist from another man. They battle for the upper hand, their hands locked. But the man looks like he's struggling the most.

Lillian changes her stance just the slightest as the man's temple starts to sweat, Lillian getting ready for the next blow. She grabs his wrist with her free hand and she thrusts his oncoming fist down before thrusting her palm into his elbow. She throws her palm into his shoulder, knocking it out of place as she keeps a hold of his wrist. She kicks him in the chest.

Lillian lets the man go and he falls to the ground. She turns around and she bends down so she's at eye level with the five-year-old girl she just defended.

"Thank you," the little girl says sweetly.

"You're welcome," Lillian replies. "And don't worry. They always try to charge women more than they should. That's when I come around."

"Can you teach me to fight like that?"

Lillian smiles at the little girl. "Of course. For you. Always."

The little girl gasps in excitement and she wraps her little arms around Lillian's neck. "Thank you! I have the biggest bully at school that needs to be taught a lesson. You're the best!"

Lillian wraps her arm around the little girl's waist. "You're welcome." She taps the little girl's back. "I teach self-defense at nine o' clock in the morning in my backyard during the summer. Tell your mom."

"I will." The little girl pulls back and looks at Lillian. "Thank you so much, Black Cat!" The smile on the little girl's face is priceless and contagious, making Lillian smile at her.

"You are *so* welcome." Lillian lightly pinches the little girl's cheek then rests her hand there. Her green eyes search the little girl's brown eyes. "Go home." She orders softly.

The little girl nods her head and she races home with the groceries that she got for her busy mom. Lillian watches the little girl run off in admiration until the little girl disappears in the distance. Lillian gets up and starts for her home, which is in the opposite direction from where the little girl went. But she gets stopped by a Viking takal with a cart being pulled by a teenaged dragon.

"I'm so sorry," Lillian says softly. She steps around the Viking to let him through. "I got in your way."

"No, no," the Viking says, his voice low and husky. "I'm in the way. I was watching you. I thought that was cute. Good of you to help the little girl out."

"I'm just doing my job to remind men of women's rights."

"And it should be pressed. My best friend's girlfriend is all about women's rights and how they should be treated as equals," the man says with a stern but soft tone.

"Do you feel the same?"

"Of course." The Viking takal lends his hand to Lillian and she looks at it. "Viggo Grimert. At your service."

"Nice to meet you, Viggo," Lillian says as she takes the man's hand in a firm grip and shakes it firmly. Her green eyes meet with his brown eyes. "I'm Lillian Carmichael."

"Are you from around here?" Viggo takes a look around his surroundings.

"Sort of." Lillian stands with her feet apart and her hands behind her back, one hand clasping her wrist. She lifts her chin as she keeps eye contact with Viggo. "I'm from Homba. This village here is in the same area as my house back home. I travel between both since I'm kind of… Part of this world, now."

A smirk spreads on Viggo's face as he realizes what Lillian means. "The Black Cat. Here in the flesh. I thought you went back to Homba after Amelia got rid of all of the spells."

"I can't stay there for very long," Lillian replies, looking down at the ground. "The cat in me starts wailing and screaming in agony inside of me and it hurts me very greatly physically if I stay there for very long." She looks up at Viggo. "If the binding spell was broken, then she would just go dormant in Homba."

"I understand that perfectly." Viggo tilts his head at Lillian, a smirk on his face. "Well, I hope you heal quickly so you can get back to your family for a bit." Lillian dips her head to Viggo. "Thank you."

"You're welcome." Viggo and Lillian part their ways and she casually walks back to her home here in Hallam. He seems to be a great man. Very caring. It lets Lillian know she can trust him. She can see why he's a potential suitor for Amari. And rightfully so! Viggo shows passion for those who can't be with their families.

Luckily for Lillian, she can bring her family here and not be completely alone. They've been accepted by Hallam as her family, but they can't stay here for very long. Lillian's husband has to go to work and her two kids have school and sports back in Homba. Lillian continues to her home here in Hallam and it doesn't take her long.

∞

Amari stands up as Ada quickly grabs her robe and towel and walks out of her bedroom, Amari doing her best to stay calm in this situation.

Allah growls when Ada's scent hits him so close and Amari is reminded of his over-protectiveness. Damn you, Ada! You just had to walk right in front of him, didn't you? Amari quickly gets her underwear and bra on as Allah glares at her, watching her get slowly dressed.

This is going to be fun! Not…

"Move any slower and you will be nailed to the wall," Allah threatens with a growl.

Amari gives Allah a smug look and she slowly zips her pants up, her button already done up.

"Oh, for fuck's sake!" Allah snaps. He takes a step towards Amari and she puts her hand up, stopping him. He respects her wish, but she can tell he doesn't want to. He wants to kill her.

She finally gets her pants all the way zipped up then she grabs her dark gray t-shirt from the ottoman. She's surprised it's still in one spot after last night! Allah growls, making everything in Ada's bedroom shake, including the floor and the walls.

"What?" Amari snaps. "What's so important? The expansion?!"

Allah points towards Amari's office, giving her a death glare. "Your office," he growls. "Now." He orders.

"I don't take orders from you." Amari shifts, stomping her foot. "You on the other hand." She points at Allah.

"Oh, don't start!" Allah snaps.

"Then. Calm! Down, Allah! You're only going to make things worse!" Amari knows she's pushing it, but she can't help herself, challenging an immortal god that can easily snap her like a twig. He's massive and towers over her as if she's just a little mouse and he's a hungry lion ready for a little snack to subdue his appetite until dinner.

Allah growls and he's slamming Amari into the wall with his hand around her throat in just a second. His silver-gray eyes glow gold as he holds back his wolf. "Don't tell me to calm down, little miss perfect." He enunciates Amari's nickname that he just gave her. "You're the one that's fucking my mate!" Allah yells in Amari's face, shaking her neck and head and making her close her eyes in fear.

"Allah. Just please try to understand. She's a lesbian!"

"I know damn fuckin' well what she is!" Allah continues to shake Amari. His breath basks her cheek threateningly and she knows she's in trouble. But she keeps it together no matter how hard Allah tries to shake her.

*Klauss, where are you?!* Amari screams in her head, hoping her desperate attempt at a mind link happens with her best friend that's bound to Hallam.

"She has that rare gene thanks to you that now I can't even touch her!"

"Just think of the bright side," Amari growls. She dares to let her brown eyes look into Allah's glowing eyes. "I have all of her eggs, now. If you ever wanted to have kids with her… Now, you can."

"Don't," Allah growls with his authoritative booming voice with Ragnar behind it and making his voice deeper. "Tempt me, wench."

"Oh, *now* you'll touch me." Great. Amari just put an idea in his head! And she knows by experience that Allah will do it!

"I don't like it as much as you do. I try to stay away from you these days. But you decided to give Madison! Hell's Fire! What the fuck is wrong with you?!"

"Hmm, let's see," Amari starts, thinking about all of her toxic traits and getting her petty on to cover up her fear. She doesn't want Allah to have the luxury to see his dominance over her working. He'll continue to torture her like this! "I'm very giving. Too caring if you ask me. I've given my heart to some people who took it, shriveled it up into nothing, and gave just one little very tiny piece back to me and making me look for all the other million pieces they tore it into."

Allah growls and tightens his grip on Amari's neck, digging his claws into it. He thrusts her head into the wall and she closes her eyes as she starts to choke.

"Don't you *dare* give Madison those papers." Allah threatens, growling the word 'dare'.

Amari grasps onto Allah's wrist, desperately trying to get out of this situation. She doesn't want to be crow food! Allah will kill her and leave her for crows and other animals to eat!

"You don't wanna kill me," she manages out in a weak voice, fighting for dominance. "You'll all-."

"We'd all be fine without you." Allah cuts Amari off. "All Selena would have to do is take your place."

"That won't work." Amari continues to struggle against Allah.

"Watch me make it work. From Hell's Fire." Allah threatens. Fuck… He's going to kill her! Fear settles in Amari's stomach and makes her sick.

*Klauss! He's going to kill me!* Amari feels a little spark of a mind link. Is he close by?! Amari prays to the God above that he is.

"Tell Madi it's not going to happen," Allah orders in an authoritative tone. "And that you'll rule Hell's Fire instead. Viggo can have Hallam."

"He's only a potential suitor. Not heir."

Standing a foot and an inch taller than Amari, Allah leans over to get in her face threateningly. Fuck. This isn't good. And Amari knows he'll do anything to get his wish.

"Change that." He snarls.

Amari shakes her head at Allah and he digs his claws deeper into her neck.

"Change it or all of Ada's eggs will be gone with you!"

Amari drops her right hand next to her side and she shifts the air in the bedroom, moving decorations and putting air between her neck and Allah's hand, making him loosen his grip a little.

"Over my dead body," she sneers.

"Fine," Allah growls. He thrusts his claws on his free hand into Amari's gut and makes her gasp in stabbing pain.

Why did she have to entice him?!

"Ada's leaving. She's coming back home. Don't try to stop us." Allah thrusts his claws out of Amari's gut and she looks down at it, watching her dark gray t-shirt get even darker with blood. Allah walks over to Ada's wardrobe.

"Not on my watch," a familiar female voice threatens. Sunni, the earth fairy that stands at five foot two inches, walks into Ada's bedroom and straight over to Amari. She catches Amari as she goes down. "I gotchu," Sunni says lowly in Amari's ear, reassuring her that everything will be alright. What is she doing here?!

Ada comes screaming in and she flings herself at Allah. "No! I'm not leaving with you!" Ada fights with Allah behind Amari and Sunni, but she's too small to even get a reaction from him.

"Stay with me, Amari," Sunni orders Amari, getting protective and healing Amari's wounds with her powers. "It's not your time. Don't fall asleep." Her voice soothes.

It calms Amari and she looks up at Sunni, her head leaning against Sunni's shoulder. Sunni keeps her arm around Amari from behind. Their eyes meet, leaf green meeting brown. "You have impeccable eyes."

"So do you." Sunni's eyes glow a deeper leaf green as she continues to heal Amari. "That's it. Keep your eyes on me."

Behind Amari and Sunni, Ada hangs on Allah's arm as he packs her suitcase with all of her clothes, never reacting to her attempts to stop him. She screams in frustration.

"You're not taking me away!" Ada screams. "I'm staying here!"

"You're not staying anywhere *near* here, Ada!" Allah barks. "You're coming home! With me! And Amari will come back in a year to give you your eggs back! You're having my pups once and for all!"

"I'll never take my eggs back!" Ada digs her heels into the wood floor, desperately trying to stop her husband, mate, and king. "They're hers, now! If you want me to have your pups! You'll have to touch Amari!"

"I'm not touching her!" Allah barks a yell, glaring at his beloved wife. His wolf howls and wreathes in agonized pain, hating this argument just as much as he does. "You're my wife! My *mate*! I will *never* touch another woman!" But he has! Has he forgotten?!

Ada looks up at Allah in fear, her blue-green eyes meeting his silver-gray eyes.

"It's you! And it's *always*! Been you! So, you better start getting used it!" All of Ada's clothes in her suitcase, Allah closes it and zips it up.

Ada lets go of him as he grabs her suitcase and starts for the door. She watches him in disbelief as she thinks about what he just said.

"Come on, Ada! Let's go!"

Mate…

Ada stares at the faded brown wood flooring that's polished. There's a reason why the word 'mate' sticks out at this very moment.

"Ada!" Allah makes Ada jump and she looks up at him. "Let's go. Please. I want you back home." With a broad god-like stature and body Allah most definitely looks the part to be the god of all were-kind. His dark gray button up shirt isn't buttoned all the way, the button at the collar open and the top button undone, showing off some of his chest hair.

If you were to unbutton one more button, you would start to see his well-toned pecks. He looks good as a sixty-seven-year-old.

Ada's eyes fill with tears, knowing what she's about to do. She has to do it. For the sake of her beliefs and Amari.

"Ada, please." Allah begs for once. "Come with me. They're all waiting for you."

"I, Ada Lyca King," Ada starts.

Allah shakes his head as fear shows in his grief-stricken eyes. "No. Ada, don't do it." He warns.

"Reject you. Allah Ammon King."

"No!" Allah starts for Ada, dropping her suitcase.

"As my mate!"

Allah falls on his knees in front of Ada as he starts to feel the pain that will keep him bed ridden until he finds his second chance mate or dies from the pain.

"And as my king! I pledge no allegiance to you no more! My heart belongs to Amari, now!"

Allah falls onto his hands and bloody tears seep from his eyes, falling on the wood floor. "Ada, no," Allah whispers.

"I suggest you do the same thing, so we don't suffer."

Allah shakes his head, looking like a crumbled up and lost puppy for once. "No." He looks up at his wife of two years. "I'll always love you." His voice shakes. "And keep you close."

"Then you'll die," Ada growls. "And I'll live. With Amari."

Allah shudders a sigh, his breath ragged. He gets up and starts out of Amari's estate, struggling to stay on his feet. Ada looks over at Amari and Sunni and rushes over to them. Amari looks up at Ada and their eyes meet as Ada gets on her knees above her.

"Hi," Ada says softly.

"Hi," Amari replies softly. "You shouldn't have done that. For me."

"I've been wanting to do that ever since he tried to touch me."

Amari sighs heavily and her breath tickles Ada's cheek.

"How are you feeling?"

"Better." Amari gets up after Sunni has sewn her up and cleaned her.

Ada looks up at her as a massive migraine starts at the back of her head. "I need to lie down. I'm starting to feel the effects of my end of the severed mate bond."

"Yes." Amari bends down and takes Ada's forearm in her hand. "Let's get you in bed. I've got some things to do, but I'll come check on you once in a while. Okay?"

Ada nods. "Okay." Ada stands up and lets Amari take her to her bed, Amari's arm around her. Ada lies down and Amari kisses her temple.

She moves Ada's bangs out of her face. "Sleep well. I'll make sure May gets you some medicine to help you with your pain."

Ada nods her head, looking up at Amari. She watches Amari walk out of her bedroom then Ada lets sleep take over her.

## 7

Amari slips away into her gardens and she stops next to the fast-growing roses and lilies. They're connected to the life back in Homba. They bloom when each baby is born and live as long as that human being, connected to it. It's a unique bond that is shared. Amari has very many flowers like this in her garden. But she didn't come out here to watch them grow.

Amari sneaks around the hedges, underneath the arch with grape vine, and past the fountain. She slips into the forest and uses a well beaten path that leads to the lycan kingdom. She knows she's being reckless. He just tried to kill her! But she knows the pain Allah is going through. She may never feel the pain since she's not a mate for any of the were-kind. None of them are potential suitors anyway.

But when a fated mate breaks the mate bond on her end and her mate doesn't accept it, he goes through excruciating pain. It's so excruciating that it usually cripples him and leads to his death.

Amari goes back to the conversation that she had with Anna when Anna tried to stop her from going after Allah to help him.

"Don't go after him," Anna had warned Amari. "You'll only make it worse."

"I have to help him," Amari said. "He's hurting."

"Yeah, but he's the lycan king. He'll kill you if you try to get too close."

Amari looked at Anna and their eyes met, standing at the same height as each other. "I just wanna help him."

Anna shook her head. "He won't see it that way."

"Then what can I do?" Amari snapped. "Leave it to Selena?"

"You might have to. He might just have to die from the pain."

"Is there any alternative?"

Anna went quiet.

"Anna, you went through the same thing when your fated mate rejected you. Did you ever…?"

"Reject him? No."

"So, how are you still standing? You should be dead."

"Usually, a rejected one will go out looking for their second chance mate if they can get through the pain. But it's hard to do. I was lucky mine was so close. The moment Caspien rejected me my second chance mate sniffed me out and found me unconscious."

"Did you…?"

Anna shook her head, catching onto what Amari was implying. "No. I would've put the pain on Caspien and then it would've been a constant battle to stay afloat."

Amari nodded her head as tears filled her eyes. She's going to have to put Ada through pain just so that Allah can get to his kingdom and start his search for his second chance mate. "So, what did your mate do instead when he found you?"

"He marked me. He felt the pull more than I did. But then again… I could hardly keep my eye opens. I just wanted to go into hibernation, so it didn't hurt so much for when I passed."

Amari nodded her head. "What about… A chosen mate. Would it work that way too?"

"Yes. But the pain doesn't stop right away like it does with a fated mate. It takes a full day to recover."

Amari walked out of her office after talking with Anna and stopped at the sound of her name, peeking back into her office with her hand on the doorframe.

"Don't go after him," Anna warned.

"I'm too busy to catch up to him at this point anyway." Amari quickly withdrew and acted natural, walking out of the front door then circling around to her gardens when no one was looking.

Amari stops when she hears a twig snap away from the path that leads to Allah's kingdom. Is there a path over there that's a shorter way there? There's only one way to find out.

∞

Allah stumbles and catches himself on the tree, holding himself up. Excruciating pain blinds him and makes his vision blurry. But he still knows where he is.

He's not taking the well beaten path between his kingdom and Amari's estate. He may be on a different path, but it's shorter. It won't take him as long to get to his kingdom.

Allah feels the mate pull and he growls, not wanting to sever his current mate bond. He's still in love with her! No matter what Ada does to him she will always be Allah's number one! Selena may have come before her. But there was no such thing as fated mates until Selena passed away and became the moon goddess.

She decided to be cruel after what happened to her, wanting to punish the were-kind that abandoned her and left her to die. Allah was out every single day, looking for her and waiting for her return. She came to him in a dream and told him what happened and what she had planned. Since she became the moon goddess no one could stop her. Except for Amari. But Amari didn't care.

*Are you happy, now, Selena? Look at me!* Silence. Allah doesn't get an answer from her. *Selena! Save me!*

Bloody tears seep down from Allah's face as he thinks about what he could've been if he didn't have a fated mate. He could've been so much more! Nothing would have made him sick! But he'll always be love stricken with Ada! No matter what she does to him!

Allah grabs the berry bush in front of him and he takes a step forward, knowing damn well it can't hold him. His weakened knees crumble and he falls to the ground. But a female arm wraps around his waist quickly and catches him before he can hit the hard earth.

"I gotchu," a familiar female voice whispers seductively in Allah's ear. No! Anyone but her! Why her?!

"Get off of me," Allah growls threateningly.

"You're hurting. Let me take care of you." Lavender and vanilla fill Allah's nostrils and Amari's scent comforts him for some reason.

"I don't want to be taken care of by you." He growls, unable to talk like a normal being towards Amari right now. His wolf howls, whines, and yelps inside of him, wanting a release.

*Take her!* No! Allah won't be taking advantage of this woman!

Amari may be the good one, but she is not Allah's friend right now! She just took his mate from him! The love of his life! Allah wanted Ada to continue to be his queen and mother of his pups!

*Get over her, Allah!* Ragnar snarls in pain. *And claim this one!*

*We are not choosing Amari!* Allah snarls at Ragnar. *We cannot! She is of different royal blood! We cannot mix together!*

*Take her or I will die!*

*I will be dying with you, brother!* Allah continues to fight with his wolf. *You're not alone!*

Ragnar wreathes in excruciating pain in silence, making Allah shiver in pain uncontrollably.  Amari shifts underneath Allah, her lips pressed into his ear. Did she say something? That's when he notices what she's doing. His limp cock out of its barrier Amari strokes his length as it slowly starts to grow.

"No!" Allah growls. Standing up with Amari's support he shoves her and she flies into the rose bush next to them. "I will not let you please me!" Allah yells as he goes down, not able to keep himself up. His knees meet the earth and Amari is right next to his side with her arm wrapped around his waist in just seconds.

"Let me help you," she coos in Allah's ear softly.

"Get your hands off me." Allah growls threateningly.

"You need a release so you can get back to your kingdom. Let me give it to you."

"I will *not* let you put Ada through that pain!"

"You think I want this? Allah? You're hurting! And you can't be left in the forest to die!"

"I will die loving and protecting my queen. Ada means *everything* to me!"

"And she loves you. Just not in that way."

Allah growls at Amari's remark. She shifts underneath him and she lays him down on the warm earth.

"What do you think you're doing?" Allah looks up at Amari and watches her.

Amari shushes him softly. "Giving you that release," she whispers.

"No!" Allah tries to stop Amari as she unbuckles her belt. But she pins him down with one hand on his chest, a threatening glare on her face.

"You're not refusing me," she says in a stern tone.

"Amari!" Allah tries to protest.

Amari puts her finger to his lips, giving him a warning look. "If you dare to say no to me one more time… I will force myself on you. And rape you." Amari threatens. "You understand me?" Amari's scent fills Allah's head, soothing and comforting him. How is she doing that?!

"Just don't put me inside of you," Allah threatens low, accepting his fate. It seems that he can't win this fight.

Amari has always been stubborn and bullheaded, trying to do the right thing. She gets it from two people. One of which is her mentor. The other is Nolan, her grandfather.

Allah watches her as she goes down on him. She takes his massive cock into her mouth. She sucks on one end of it as it continues to grow a few more inches and strokes it from the middle of it and to the hilt. Her touch sends comfort and ease through Allah's body and he watches her as she deep throats him, only able to go half way with how thick and long he is.

He groans as pleasure sweeps through him and starts to take away his pain, laying his head back and looking up at the clear, bright sky. He shouldn't be letting her do this! The pain is transferring to Ada! And that's the last thing he wants! Amari, of all people, should know how he feels! She's been there! But for some reason she's helping him, something tugging them towards each other.

Allah has always admired Amari, but he could never touch her in the seductive manner. Not even when he was with his first wife, Selena. But then there was that night a week after she passed… Allah shudders at the memory.

Amari chokes, indicating she's still deep throating Allah's cock. It excites him and he starts to feel a familiar pull. His hand instantly goes to Amari's head and his fingers interlace with her dark, golden-brown hair. He doesn't force her down on him, but he doesn't just let her guide herself either.

His hand goes with the motion of her head and when she deep throats him, he forces her to stay there and thrusts his cock deeper into her throat, making her choke as if she's gasping for air for the life of her. Allah groans and pulls his hips back, keeping Amari's head in place. She doesn't move and he thrusts his cock down her throat, again, past her gag reflex and making her choke for air, again.

He growls at her throat tightening around him and he looks down at her, her hand pressed against her lips at his hilt.

"That's right," Allah growls, able to think clearly for a moment. "Succumb to me, you little wench." He pulls his hips back then thrusts his cock down Amari's throat, making her choke for air for the third time.

She tries to breathe through her nose, but it's no use. Allah throws his head back in pleasure. This is so wrong. But he can't stop himself at this point.

Amari pulls her mouth off of Allah's cock, but she still strokes it with her hand. Allah hears some rustling and a moment later Amari is straddling his broad hips and frame. Oh, no she doesn't.

Amari rips Allah's gray button-up shirt open and her lips land on his pecks. She licks his nipple then pulls it into her mouth, sucking on it and flicking it with her tongue.

Allah growls, Amari stroking his cock at a slow pace while also sucking on his nipple. She lets go of his nipple after marking him there, making a small popping sound, and then she trails her lips up Allah's chest and to his neck. Her lips stop where his mate mark has started to disappear and she kisses it tenderly. She lets her breath mingle there and tickle his skin. He grunts at the sensation. This is so wrong, but Allah can't stop Amari.

Ragnar starts howling in delight in Allah's head and there's only one reason for him to do that. Allah furrows his brows as Amari's lips trail up his neck and across his square jaw. He clenches it as it all starts to come together. Her touch… The pull… The pain…

Amari's lips land on Allah's lips and he thrusts her back, making their eyes meet.

"Don't," he growls warningly, unable to threaten her at this point. It's not true! This can't be true! Could it?

"Very well, then," Amari breathes. She sits up and Allah looks up at the sky.

He can't continue this! Not because of Ada! She's not feeling any of it! The betrayal or the pain! Allah just can't continue, because it will secure the mate bond! And he's still in love with Ada!

"Ada, forgive me," Amari growls softly.

Wait… "What?" Allah looks up at Amari to see her fully naked and readying herself over Allah. "No!" He grabs her hips, stopping her, and their eyes meet. Gray meets brown as fear sweeps over him. "You don't understand."

Amari nods her head. "I think I do."

"Amari. No!" Allah gets cut off as Amari falls on top of him and takes him in completely, guiding his cock deep inside of her and the hilt pressing into her vulva.

"Uh!" Amari drawls out, throwing her head back in pleasure and closing her eyes. "Fuck!" She and Allah are going to Hell's Fire for this!

Good, Goddess. They're in trouble, now! The mate bond being confirmed, Allah can only think of doing one thing. He sits up and towers over Amari, who sits in his lap while straddling him. His arms go around her and he presses her naked breasts into the top of his naked rib cage.

Her hands instantly push his shirt back and toss it aside. Her arms wrap around his neck and she pulls his head in towards her. His lips land on her jaw line and there's only one thing he can think of doing. Intensifying the mate bond. Allah holds onto Amari's hips and he thrusts into her. She gasps in pleasure and holds him even closer.

"Allah," Amari says, her voice filled with lust. "Fuck. Allah!"

At the sound of his name, Allah growls into Amari's ear and lays her down on the ground, keeping himself completely inside of her. Her tightness pulses around him and pulls him in, accepting him as her mate. Amari gasps in pleasure from the sensation and starts panting.

Allah pulls her hips towards him, making them equivalent with his. Then he thrusts into her, making her gasp with every thrust and pant. He thrusts into her harder with every thrust and makes her breasts bounce harder with every thrust. If they were in a bed, the headboard would be banging against the wall.

"Ah," Amari moans in pleasure. She rolls on top of Allah as their senses heighten and he watches her as she rides him. Apparently, she's not done with him. Allah holds onto Amari's hips. Every time she comes down on him, he thrusts into her and gets her spot every time, making her orgasm. She's so beautiful when she orgasms. And he wants to make her do it more.

He's done this with her once before, but in her dream. At the reminder, Allah groans, wanting his release. He knows Amari has every single one of Ada's eggs and he decides to impregnate one of them, making Amari deliver Ada's baby just this one time.

Next year or the year after, he'll impregnate one of Ada's eggs inside of Amari again and have her shoot it into Ada so Ada can carry instead. It's a good plan. And a win, win for both of them. Ada carries Allah's pups and rules beside him. And Amari gets to keep her mistress. This is the only way Allah will accept Amari as part of Ada's sex life. Even if Ada doesn't want him anymore.

Amari comes down on Allah and he thrusts into her, making her eyes roll to the back of her head as it hangs in front of her, her hair falling in front of her face. Allah reaches up and tucks Amari's hair behind her ear and she looks at him with a soft surprised look.

Brown eyes meet gray eyes and a message is sent between them without them having to speak a word. Their mating bond stays a secret. No one can know. Amari's brown eyes turn softer and she lowers herself on top of Allah, keeping their eyes locked. Amari kisses Allah's chest tenderly and he rolls on top of her. Her arms wrap around his torso with her hands on his shoulders.

Her thighs wrap around his waist and her calves press into his naked backside. Allah thrusts into Amari and Ragnar growls.

*Finish her!*

His senses heightened, he trails his hand down Amari's side then pulls her into him, her hips pressed into his hips and her breasts flush with his rib cage. He holds her pressed against him like this and puts his free hand flat on the ground above his head. Allah takes his time, thrusting into Amari and letting her orgasm at every thrust. The mate bond is only going to grow stronger every time they do it, their senses heightened even more each time.

Soon, they won't be able to get enough of each other and will give into their mate bond, marking each other and claiming their thrones beside each other. They'll be unstoppable and no one will be able to get in between them.

"Faster," Amari whispers near Allah's ear seductively.

He obeys her order for once and gives into the pleasure enveloping him. Allah thrusts into Amari so fast and hard his wolf speed kicks in and Amari can't stop voicing her moans, grunts, and groans. She clings onto Allah and her nails dig into his shoulders. He curls his nails into the dirt as he starts to get close to his own release, her tightness enveloping him.

"Ah," Amari lets out in a high pitch. "Huh. Ah, ah, ah." Her voice staccato with every thrust Amari can't stop, having orgasm after orgasm. "Allah!"

He growls into her hair, his testicles tightening. He's almost there… He's almost there!
"Fuck! Allah!"

At the sound of his name on her tongue, Allah's testicles jump and he thrusts into Amari super hard one last time. He stills his hips as he keeps himself buried inside of her. She clings onto him, almost choking him as her orgasm gets heightened, and he spills his seed inside of her.

Please let it be one of Ada's eggs! Sweat rolls down Allah's temple and he looks down at Amari. He watches her slowly come back to him after having an orgasm, shaking in his arms. Allah gets protective of Amari and he holds her close. This is the start of a new relationship between them. One that involves her giving him pups whether it be with Ada's eggs or her eggs.

Amari pants as she holds onto Allah and he waits until she's ready to talk to him. A branch snaps in the distance.

"Shift," Amari says lowly.

"What?" Allah doesn't want to leave yet! His wolf is just starting to celebrate!

Amari turns her head to look at him. "Shift. Now."

"Why?"

"Do you want us to get caught?"

"Only if you want to." Allah flirts.

"That'd be bad for the both of us." Amari pushes on Allah and he takes her with him as he stands up. He lets her down and she stands on her own two feet, completely naked with a few twigs in her hair.

"I'll see you tonight?"

"No. I got some paperwork to take care of. With both coronations and everything else."

"Here," Allah says softly. He takes the twigs out of Amari's hair.

She looks to see what he pulled out. "Thanks." She looks up at him. "I'll see you at my crowning on Saturday."

"But what about beforehand? Surely, you can't be that busy."

"Believe or not I have in image to uphold, Allah. If I'm seen with you, everybody is gonna know something's up."

"I know it doesn't look good for us." Allah looks down and pulls his pants and boxers over his buttocks. He arranges his limp cock in his boxers then looks at Amari as he zips up his pants. "But believe it or not I wanna start seeing you." Allah speaks softly, being sincere since he's starting to think about it. "You're my second chance mate after all."

"And the moment someone sees us like this and knows that Ada is only suffering a migraine and aching limbs," Amari starts as she gets closer to Allah and sets her hand on his abs. She keeps her eyes on him, looking up at him since he's a foot and an inch taller than her.

Her potential and rightful suitor Viggo is just an inch shorter than him.

"They'll all be coming to your kingdom with a vengeance for your head," Amari warns lowly. "So, go." Still in love with Ada but wanting Amari as well,

Allah breathes in through his nose as he brings his lips to Amari's. Her lips melt into his and he wraps his arms around the middle of her torso, rubbing her sides seductively.

Oh, he wants to do it with her tonight. Allah breathes Amari's scent through his nose, lavender and vanilla filling his nostrils. He opens his mouth, so her scent hits his scent glands as well. If he can't see her until her crowning, her scent will have to do the next few days.

"I'll come check on you on Thursday," Amari whispers into Allah's mouth, their breaths mingling together. She trails her hand up his chest. "Now, shift."

Even though it already pains him, Allah takes a few steps back away from Amari. The feel of her hand on his chest never leaves as his silver-gray eyes meet her brown eyes. He gives her a small smirk.

"I'll see you Thursday," he says lowly. Allah lets Ragnar take over and he shifts.

Ragnar stands tall and proud on all four paws as he shakes his head, completely healed and ready to take on anything. Small hands run through his silver fur and his gold eyes look at Amari. He smells something inside of her that's waiting to be woken up and he's drawn to it.

Amari takes a step back and lets her brown eyes meet Ragnar's gold eyes with a smirk on her face.

"I've always wanted to feel your fur, Ragnar," Amari says softly, admiration dripping into her voice. She takes another step back and motions her chin at the trail that's the least taken, but also the shortest route to Allah's kingdom. Her eyes land on Ragnar lovingly.

"Go."

Ragnar dips his head then takes off for his kingdom on the trail. *There's something inside of her*, Ragnar says to Allah.

*Like what?* Allah replies.

*Like… I don't know. But it's something that's waiting to be woken up.*

*Well, we're going to have to wake it up*, Allah says with a smirk.

Ragnar pants at the thought, hoping that happens soon.

8

Amari watches Allah run off in wolf form with admiration. She knows he usually hates her. She's always the bearer of bad news. But now it's different. She's not so sure about the mate bond, but she's grateful Allah didn't mark her. If he did, they would've been in deep shit. And they don't want any trouble with Hallam.

Most of the creatures here have a problem with Madi as it is! She's killed very many in her dreams, killing almost half the population here. All the lieuts are now extinct! And who knows if the werecats have been having any! A lieut is practically a werecat but without a human form. It's the offspring of werecats when they're mating in cat form. When they're in labor and just about to give birth to the creature they're unexpectedly forced into cat form. The cat form is the only way to bare a lieut.

But werecats don't ever do that anymore. They enjoy the sex in human form anymore. Lieuts… They're so cute when they're just cubs! Amari is a cat lover and she enjoys having Raja as her fighting companion.

Hmm… Where is Raja? Amari hasn't seen her since she's crossed over. Amari's mind goes back to Allah and she can picture him just now. He was so good with a litter of lieut cubs when their mother was killed by one of his own.

She was just protecting her babies when the brute came striding through the forest, looking for a poor creature to relieve on. That brute never likes to mate in human form or with his own kind. He forces himself on just about every creature that crosses his path. When a momma lieut was startled by his crashing through the forest with no care in the world but to kill her babies and make her bare his hybrids.

Allah killed his own lycan to save what he could, the momma lieut already in a pool of her own blood.

"Hmm," Amari moans as she sighs and goes back to her dream of watching Allah with the cubs, bottle feeding them and loving them as if they were his own. He'd make a great father someday.

It's a shame Ada was born with the rare gene. She would've been straight or bi if it weren't for the gene and she would've been able to give Allah pups with no problem! What really intrigues Amari is why the rare gene makes women into lesbians.

It'll always be a mystery to her as she never dreamed a reason for it. And she has no idea what to call the gene! Amari moans, wanting to give Allah Ada's pups, but she can't. Not as of this moment. Pups… Amari cringes. Fuck!

"I need to pee," Amari whispers. She quickly grabs her clothes and Allah's torn clothes.

He really shouldn't have put those jeans back on. And they looked *so* good on him! Amari quickly gets her underwear top, bra, and t-shirt on as she gets behind a bush and squats. She leans back into the tree behind her and she relieves herself, not wanting to get pregnant.

Besides! It's her eggs for the next few rounds since Ada gave them back to her in the end! Amari's got to be careful!

*Not so clever, was she,* a female voice says in Amari's head, scaring her.

Amari screams.

*Sorry, Amari. It's me.*

Amari relaxes as a wind picks up and honeysuckle and vanilla blows in the breeze. Selena. Amari lays her head back against the tree and looks up at the leaves and the bright blue sky. "Who wasn't so clever?"

*Ada. She gave you your eggs back.*

"She just doesn't want to be stuck with any right now. She's traumatized somehow."

*She's not traumatized. She just wants revenge.*

"Hmm," Amari moans.

*But she doesn't know that you're Allah's second chance mate.*

"Why am I?" Amari waits a moment, not bothering to put her underwear and pants on yet since she wants to dry out first. "Allah's second chance mate? You know Hallam is gonna kill him once they find out."

*They need the change.*

Amari sighs in frustration and lifts her head. "You and I have different ideas in change."

"Huh," a familiar male voice asks.

Amari looks at the man on the other side of the bush and she knows he's looking for her. "What?"

"What?"

"Klauss! What are you doing out here?!"

"Looking for you." Klauss narrows his ocean blue eyes at Amari. "What are you doing out here? And what are you doing behind that bush?!"

"I had to pee." Amari grabs her underwear and gets it on. Then she gets her pants on.

"You couldn't wait?!"

"I was coming back from Allah's kingdom after getting him in the safety of his walls. He couldn't stay out here. Ada just rejected him."

"That explains why you reek of him."

"Oh, boohoo!" Amari zips her pants up then starts buckling up her belt. "So, I reek of him. Doesn't give you the right to complain."

"Did he…?"

Amari glares up at her best friend. She hates being short at times like these.

"You know."

Amari shakes her head at Klauss and he sighs and sags, letting his hands down and putting his blades back into his arms. His swords disappear as well.

"Fuck you! Did he put his cock… Inside of you?!"

Amari winces with the deepest glare she can manage in acted disgust. "Fuck no! He hates me as it is! Why would he…?"

"Well, then how would you explain that?!" Klauss points at Amari's neck and her hand instantly flies to the tender spot that usually gets a mate mark.

Did Allah really mark her without her knowing?

"Made you flinch." Klauss smirks at Amari.

"Ooo! You are just…" Amari picks up Allah's button up shirt that has no more buttons and his completely shredded boxers and pants. "Full of it today!"

"Hey," Klauss snaps. "I just about lost my best friend today!"

Amari shifts the air and camouflages Allah's clothes as a torn-up bag, waving her hand over them. She steps out from behind the bush.

"I get to have a little fun after that scare! Okay?!"

"You rushed here, didn't you?"

"You think?! God… Amari!" Klauss turns to face Amari, keeping his eyes on her.

She walks up to him as he watches her.

"I get a mind link for the first time and it's from you! Telling me that he's going to *kill* you? The only male I could think of that would *dare* to do such a thing is Allah! I could've lost you, Amari," Klauss breathes softly. "And I would've if Sunni didn't hear your mind link as well! Do you know how scary that was?" Klauss's blue eyes show grief and Amari knows he's not just talking about her. He lost his mom not too long ago when nobody listened to the cries of her grimmal.

"I'm so sorry, Klauss," Amari whispers. "I know how you must feel right now."

Klauss leans over, getting eye level with Amari and sneaking his hand around her neck to entangle his fingers in her dark, golden-brown hair. He lets her see the fear that he felt just moments ago. "I am not… Letting you out of my sight, Amari. You're my best friend. And I can't afford to lose you, too."

Amari nods her head. "Okay," she whispers. She looks down at the ground.

"And get rid of the disguise on what you're holding. It reeks of Allah more than you do."

Amari looks at Klauss in true fear, truly afraid of how he will react over Allah's ripped clothes. Klauss searches Amari's eyes.

"You had sex with him. Didn't you?"

"What?" Amari shakes her head and searches Klauss's eyes, looking for a way out of this conversation. But she fails.

"Didn't you?" He presses.

"Klauss, I…"

"Get rid of the disguise." Klauss orders.

Amari sighs with a shudder, tears in her eyes. She can't ignore the order from her future takal king. She glides her hand palm down over Allah's ripped clothes and Klauss looks at them in horror, his eyes going wild for not a good reason.

"Amari, what did you do," Klauss growls. He looks at Amari with a concerned glare and she knows exactly why he's so concerned.

"He was in pain."

"Are you his second chance mate?" Klauss asks lowly.

"He *had* to get to his kingdom." Amari takes a step towards Klauss. "Fast. So he can find her."

"He was able to shift. Amari." Klauss presses. "I saw him. Every creature here knows were-creatures can't shift when their creature is trying to heal for the little bit of time they have before the pain comes back!"

Fuck. This isn't looking good for Amari.

"Did you mark him?!" Klauss presses in a booming voice.

Amari shakes. She hates seeing him like this! "No."

"Are you sure?! He could have your mark without you knowing! You have that effect!"

"I promise." Amari lifts her chin and meets her best friend's eyes. "I did not mark him."

Klauss takes a step closer to Amari and points at her, knowing damn well what's going on. "You're his second chance mate."

"Klauss…" Amari watches Klauss as he starts for her estate. "Wait." She calls.

"If I were to walk into Ada's room, right now," Klauss starts. He stops and turns to look back at Amari. "Would she be in bed because of her migraine and aches and pains? Or will she be up and about because she found her second chance mate?"

"Klauss, you know I'm only allowed to be the second chance mate for just one," Amari calls out as Klauss continues to start for her estate.

"Yeah, well, I wouldn't be surprised if you're fated for two!"

Amari winces and tears threaten to fall down her face.

"Come on! We got a secret to keep and we need a plan of attack!"

Relief floods through Amari instantly, a tear escaping her right eye. Thank, Thor. Not that Amari believes in paganism. She's a Mormon Christian! But nobody would know that since she always takes care of her urges. And she tends to have a drink. Amari takes a step forward and she tells herself she can do this. It's Klauss! He's totally reasonable!

∞

Allah gets out of the shower and grabs his towel. He dries himself as thoughts of Amari hit him, again. The way she felt… Her skin pressed against his skin. Her breath mingling on the spot that had his mate mark…

Amari is so intoxicating and there's nothing Allah can do about it. He has to stay away from her. For the sake of his kingdom. If he's seen with her, suspicions are going to be made. He already had to come up with a reason to his people why he smelt like her. He tried to act like he was in pain, said that Amari brought him here. But for the first time everybody saw through his act.

Allah walks out of his luxurious bathroom, wrapping his towel around his waist and securing it, and into his luxurious bedroom. He could keep his pups and wife in here with him with how big the bedroom is!

Allah walks over to his long dresser and opens the drawer with his boxers. That's when it happens. The memory of Amari's body entering his mind as the pain hits him in the chest.

"Fuck," Allah whispers. He grasps onto his dresser and his knuckles turn white. He can hear them. Amari and Ada making love just so Amari can release Ada from her pain sooner. He can hear them moaning. Groaning. Squealing and growling as Amari thrusts her pelvis into Ada's with a strap-on attached to her.

Allah can see them. Hear their skin slapping as they drive each other to their ecstasy. Their lips fuse together in his mind with Ada on top of Amari. Amari holding onto Ada's hips and driving that stupid small dildo into her opening while an even smaller one drives into Amari's opening at a different angle on the strap-on. Allah's testicles jump at the thought of his women doing it together and he slams his fist into his dresser, cracking it evenly.

He growls. Amari is not his woman! She's off limits! But yet… The way that he's starting to feel about her is starting to take over him, clouding some of his judgement.

*Look up, Allah.* Ragnar speaks to Allah in a voice of concern.

"No," Allah growls, trying to control the pain that he feels. His hair tickles his eyelids as he gets thrown into another scene.

Amari rolls on top of Ada and picks up the speed, thrusting into Ada so hard the headboard is banging against the wall. Their cries and sounds of pleasure fill

Allah's ears and head and he can't get them out. Ada caresses Amari's side and thrusts Amari into her, their breasts flush together so much so they're flat against each other's chest.

"Amari," Ada says out loud, her voice filled with lust and pleasure while echoing Amari's name in Allah's head.

He flinches at the sound and growls constantly as he tries to get Ada and Amari out of his head. "Amari."

"Uh," Ada moans in pleasure in a high-pitch, her head thrown back with Amari's lips on the spot that once had Allah's mark. Why is she doing this?

"Don't you fuckin' dare," Allah growls, threatening Amari not to leave her mark on Ada. Why can't he get her out of his head?!

Yes, Amari is Allah's second chance mate. But he doesn't want to think about her all the time! He's got better things to do! Amari. The memory of her body pressed against Allah's comes back into his mind and his cock grows hard. Thinking about punishing her in bed, Ragnar gets excited.

*Look up, you idiot!*

Allah instantly listens to Ragnar's command and he looks into the mirror in front of him. A mate mark shows on the spot on the left side of Allah's neck. Gold wings shine bright behind a golden wolf's head.

"Fuck, Amari." Allah thrusts his towel off of his waist and chucks it to the floor. "We agreed. To no mate marks!" He puts his fists on the top of his sleek, dark wood dresser and leans into it, staring at the mate mark. He has to admit it's pretty impressive! Gold wings are a nice touch. But this is not okay.

"Fine," Allah growls. "If this is how you're gonna play…" He mind links with his favorite omega, who used to be his mistress until Ada came along. He's having fun with her to get back at Amari.

*Amy, come to my bedroom. Now!* He orders in the mind link. If this is how Amari is going to be, Allah can keep up with her.

Besides… This is a game that two can play.

∞

Amari walks out of the bathroom, braiding her hair with her towel wrapped around her body. Garrett looks up from his Tom Clancy novel and watches her as she walks over to her rustic farmhouse dresser. She opens the top drawer and looks for bottoms and a top of her white garments, her Mormon underwear.

"You're staring," Amari says as she finds a top, feeling Garrett's eyes on her. "What's up?" She sets the top garment on her dresser.

"You," Garrett replies.

Amari finds a pair of bottoms and she sets the pair of a top and bottoms on the top of the dresser before closing the drawer. "What about me?"

"Well, first… I wasn't here to protect you when Allah attacked you. Sunni and Ada came to the rescue. Your mistress and earth fairy."

"Yeah. And?"

"And then when Ada severed her end of the mate bond with him, which by the way you messed with the wrong person."

"That was my bad. I had no idea."

"Yeah. Neither did I." Garrett puts his book down and Amari can feel his eyes burning into her skull. "How did we miss that?"

"I don't know. You tell me. But anyway." Amari grabs a big t-shirt that she got as a hand-me-down from one of her guy friend's mom. "As you were saying about me."

"Well… You went after the guy! And you made sure he got to his kingdom when he stabbed you right in the liver with his claws! You should've died, Amari!"

"I had Sunni."

"Yeah. You're lucky, by the way. That she heard your mind link that was meant for Klauss. How did you know he was close by?"

"I didn't. I just tried to reach out to him."

"Well, Klauss told me everything. You're very brave to face the man."

"Thank you. I take that as a compliment." A wave of pain hits Amari's gut and she doubles over on her dresser. This isn't cramps or bloating. No. This is much worse! But how? And why?

Amari tries to act natural in front of Garrett, knowing there's something going on. *Klauss, can you hear me?* Amari mind links with Klauss as the pain takes over her whole entire body.

*Yeah, what's up?* Klauss connects to Amari.

*How far away would you say Allah is from here?*

*I'd say…* Klauss cuts off the mind link for a moment.

Amari closes her eyes and grips onto her dresser.

"Amari, are you okay," Garrett asks.

"Yeah. I'm fine." Amari manages out casually. Her grip on her dresser tightens as the pain intensifies. What the fuck is going on? Why does she feel all this pain?

*Ten miles from here,* Klauss finally replies.

*How far can a mind link go?* Amari stretches her foot and acts like she's got a foot cramp, so Garrett doesn't suspect a thing.

*Ten miles. Why?*

*No reason. I just need to converse with him.*

*He better not be fucking that omega of his or I'm gonna kill him,* Klauss growls, sounding overly protective.

That must be it! Amari bites on her bottom lip as she waits for the pain to ease. She cuts off the mind link with Klauss. Garrett is next to her as she dances her feet as if one is cramping very badly.

"Here," Garrett whispers. "Let me take you to the bed and massage your feet. Get that cramp out."

Amari nods her head, her eyes closed. "Mhmm." She lets Garrett pick her up bridal style and carry her to the bed.

"Right in the middle?"

"Yeah." Amari whispers. The pain doesn't stop. She wishes it would. She's going to have to have a talk with Allah.

Garrett lays Amari down on her side of the bed and sits at her feet. He grabs her left foot, the one she acted like was cramping and starts to rub it right in the middle. For some reason the rubbing helps ease the pain and Amari is able to relax, sinking into the bed.

"It's all the sitting you did at home and then walking ten miles to Allah's kingdom with all of his weight on you," Garrett puts in low as he continues to rub Amari's foot, looking at her.

"I couldn't just leave him in the forest, Garrett," Amari replies, able to relax with his rubbing. Someone tries to mind link with her. It's foreign, but yet familiar.

Having a good idea on who it is, Amari cuts off the mind link before Allah can try to talk to her.

"Amari," Garrett puts in.

"Huh? What?"

"I just asked you a question."

"Sorry. I was conversing with Klauss in a mind link." She lies, not wanting Garrett to get suspicious. She doesn't want to break his heart for what she did for Allah, either. She didn't know how he would react.

He's been in love with her for quite some time. Amari wasn't about to make things bad between her and the man she so loved. She hates that she's such a giving person.

"Makes sense. He travelled all this way as fast as he could for your crowning. Hasn't had a wink of sleep the past two days."

"Poor guy. He needs to rest."

"Yeah," Garrett drawls out. "Hopefully he'll be able to switch it off with the time difference."

Amari lifts her other foot and wiggles her toes for Garrett to take it and start massaging. He switches her feet, putting her left one down on the bed and grabbing her other. "Um. Iceland… Right? That's where his people technically are?"

"Sweden. Actually."

"Oh. Yeah." Amari sighs and relaxes into her bed. "What was your question earlier?"

"Are you going to go visit Allah to see how he's doing?"

"Of course!" Allah tries to mind link with Amari, again. But she cuts it off. "He may be an ass sometimes. But really, he's just over-protective."

"That's what you said about Mike at first. But now you say he's an acquired taste."

"That nephew of yours is messed up." Amari looks at Garrett and their eyes meet.

That's when an earthquake begins, throwing everybody in Hallam off. What the fuck? People don't just get sucked into Hallam! The axis might be off, but Hallam went to smaller earthquakes that you can't feel! It's when someone that doesn't belong here or in Homba crosses over! But not everyone gets the power to do that! It's only Amari, Garrett, Adam, and Lillian that have the power! After looking around at the shaking bedroom Amari's and Garrett's concerned gazes meet each other.

"Someone's here," Amari mumbles after the earthquake stops.

"Yep," Garrett drawls out. He quickly gets up. "We've gotta find them."

"Jarom would know." Amari sat up.

Garrett looks at her. "Well, then… What are you waiting for? Use the mind link and find out!"

"Give me a second to recuperate."

"My bad," Garrett drags out, being over dramatic. He turns his back to Amari as he gets dressed.

*Jarom!* Amari sends out the mind link. *Who's here?!*

Silence. Jarom doesn't reach out in the mind link.

*Jarom?* Amari waits a few minutes for a reply, lying in bed in silence.

*I don't know,* Jarom finally replies. *I can't... I can't find them!*

*Raja, what about you? Anything?*

Raja is quiet, but Amari can feel her pacing in her chambers. She knows... And she's not very happy about how it happened.

*Raja, talk me!*

*It's Kera!* Raja roars. *She escaped Hell's Fire! We need more cats! Now!*

Amari's eyes race from side to side as she tries to come up with a plan. She can't dream about more cats on demand! How is she going to create more?! She doesn't know how here! Not just yet! She still has yet to figure it out!

*Who did she take, Raja? Kera. She took someone from Homba!*

*I know!* Raja stops pacing and starts growling. *And you're not gonna like who she took.*

*Who?!* Amari replies.

*Michael Carr.*

Amari looks at Garrett. "Kera has your nephew."

*Amari!* Raja roars.

*What?!* Amari looks at the foot of the bed, focusing on her companion.

*We need more cats! Now!*

*I don't know how!*

Raja roars out in frustration and Hallam feels it. She cuts off the mind link right away. Shit…

This is bad.

# Code

## 9

Allah shifts into human form after running through the forest in wolf form. He quickly gets a pair of pants on as he walks through Amari's gardens.

Her first call has been sent and Allah had to make sure Ada is safe. She's not an omega, but she hasn't been training as a warrior since she ran off to become one of Amari's maids two years ago. Right after Ada and Allah got married and he tried to take her to bed. She was just seventeen. He thought that maybe she was just intimidated. But no. She's a lesbian with the rare gene. He's taking her back to his kingdom where she can be kept safe. She's not staying here!

Allah steps through the back door of Amari's estate and everything is hectic. Maids are changing into sports bras and sweatpants in their quarters and the manservants are dressed in gym shorts and grabbing emergency supplies. One of them walks out of a secret room behind the dining room with a duffel bag and Allah guesses that's the storage room. He peers in to have his assumptions supported. Allah walks into the maids' quarters and starts for Ada's bedroom.

"She's not in there," one of the maids barks.

Allah doesn't listen and he kicks the door in after discovering it's locked. A manservant is kissing and getting dirty with a maid. But he jumps back at the sudden interruption.

"Dude," the manservant barks, glaring at Allah. "Privacy!"

"Where's Ada," Allah presses.

"With Queen Amari! Now, get out of here! I'm trying to bid my wife and mate goodbye!"

Allah growls at the manservant to gain dominance, but it doesn't work.

"Your powers don't work here! Amari is in charge. Not you!"

"Put your clothes back on and get back to work," Allah orders lowly. He picks up the door and puts it back on the doorway.

He walks out of the maids' quarters and catches a manservant that's trying to evacuate everybody, grabbing him by the collar of his cotton gray t-shirt. The manservant's dirty blond hair is nicely trimmed and professional looking. He looks important!

"Hey," Allah mumbles, grabbing the man's attention. "Where's Amari?"

"Right behind you," the manservant replies. His green eyes glow purple. Wait… He's a were-cat! "Amari, your boyfriend's here!" The man calls around Allah's shoulder.

"Thank you, Xander," Amari says in an orderly fashion.

The were-cat slips out of the lycan king's hold and Allah looks back at Amari, Ada behind her at the staircase holding onto another woman that she seems so in love with already. Allah knows that woman…

"You look well for a dead man," a manservant says as he squeezes past Allah. It's the manservant that was trying to get it on with the maid just a moment ago!

Allah looks at the manservant. "Second chance mate. I didn't ask for her to come along."

"Yeah?" The manservant walks backwards as he gets closer to Amari, who is peeking into the kitchen and talking to one of the cooks in an authoritative tone. "Well, maybe you should be more grateful."

"Watch your mouth, punk," Allah threatens with a growl.

The manservant shakes his head, his black-haired perm bouncing on the top of his head while he has the sides shaved. "Amari." He grabs his lady's attention by just saying her name and standing a little too close to her for Allah's liking. He may not like her much at times like these, but she was still his mate. "We got the villages here covered with some of the lycan king's best warriors. They just arrived in the village down south and a few are almost at the two on both borders. Do you want us calling the shot?"

Amari looks at her manservant. "No. Lycans are big pushovers. They won't listen to you."

"Hey," Allah defends himself, his brows furrowed. Amari glances at him.

"No offense."

"Offense taken anyway!"

Amari moans in disgust and looks at her manservant, having no idea Allah can hear her over the noise with his lycan hearing. She takes something out of her pocket, wearing high-waisted workout pants and a tank top.

Well, that's new! Allah has never seen her in something like that before! Amari hands something to her manservant.

"Manny, I want you to report to your pack. I know they rejected you, but they'll listen to you since you're one of my best."

The manservant nods his head. "Okay."

"Give this to the alpha. She'll know what to do with it."

"Okay. Sounds good." Manny, the servant, starts for the back door.

"Oh, and, Manny!"

"Yeah!" Manny turns around and lifts his chin, looking at Amari.

"Amiah Keen."

Manny smiles and walks past Allah, bumping him in the process. "That's my girl!"

Allah sighs and sags in frustration. He can see why Manny's pack rejected him! He's such a pushover! Amari exchanges something with a cook then starts towards Allah.

"Code nine," Amari says in her warning call. She sounds normal here. But all-around Hallam her voice is booming for everyone to hear. "Villagers, please stay inside your homes with your families and pets. And lock your doors. Secure your livestock and make sure nothing can get in. Or out. Warriors, I need you at your stations. Every village must be protected. All livestock must be out of harm's way. And all riders must be with their companion. We must be ready to defend what is ours. This is not a drill. This is code nine." Amari starts to walk past Allah after confirming some things with her people and he grabs her upper arm.

Allah quickly takes Amari with him and he leads her to her office, which is almost completely bare of everything. Books are missing from the bookshelves and the desk and chair are nowhere to be found.

"What is wrong with you," Allah snaps quietly. He knows Amari's office is soundproof, but one could never be too careful.

"What do you mean what's wrong me? What's wrong with you?! Putting me through that pain just moments ago!"

"You put me through it first, Amari! I told you to stay the fuck away from Ada!"

"I wasn't releasing her!"

"Then who was?!"

"Her second chance mate. They always felt a pull towards each other here in my estate. But it wasn't until she broke it with you that May was pulled to her bedroom!"

"Then who were you doing earlier?" Allah takes a threatening step towards Amari.

She crosses her arms in front of her breasts with an eyebrow raised. "You." She drawls out.

"After that, Amari! You did it with someone!"

"Oh," Amari drawls out. She points at Allah. "You mean the quickie I had with the new happy couple. Long story short." Amari lays her arm across her other arm with a smug look on her face. "I won."

Allah growls and thrusts Amari into the empty bookshelf next to them. It rocks and it sounds like it's not empty at all. "What the fuck, Amari?" He snaps.

She lifts her chin, her eyes meeting Allah's. "An illusion thanks to Ada. Nobody will think we're home." Amari sneers, sounding proud of herself. She shouldn't be. She marked Allah earlier!

"That's not what I'm talking about!" Allah barks.

"Then enlighten me." Amari doesn't sound amused. "Because you're looking super-hot right now. Is that a new shirt?" Amari flirts sarcastically.

Allah thrusts his fist into the bookshelf right next to Amari's head, making a hole.

"Great. Now, Ada has to do the magic spell to hold that."

"Listen to me, you little wench," Allah growls with a snarl, glaring at Amari. "I'll play your games. But you're not touching Ada, again. You understand me?!"

"No. Because as far as I'm concerned. She's filing for a divorce."

Allah throws his other fist back, his teeth clenched.

"Uh. Uh. Uh." Amari wags her finger at Allah, making him stop and wanting to obey her. Why does she have this effect on him? "Put another hole in my estate and you're paying for the damage."

"Fine," Allah growls. He takes a step back from Amari, hoping her soothing but intoxicating scent won't take effect on him.

"I got matters to attend to," Amari mumbles.

"I'm not done with you," Allah threatens as he grabs Amari's arm and keeps her from leaving. He wasn't letting her get away this time!

She looks up at him and their eyes clash. Her sweet scent fills Allah's nostrils and all he wants to do is take her over her desk and lock her in her office, making sure that she doesn't ever touch Ada, again.

Since he discovered she marked him earlier his mindset has changed all over, again. And he wants to punish her for what she did. They had a fucking agreement! It may not have been said out loud, but it was sent between them nevertheless!

Allah leans his face down towards Amari's face in a threatening motion, making sure she gets the message.

"I'm not yours to claim," Allah threatens. Even though he'd like her to claim him, he's not happy about the mate mark.

Although, Ragnar seemed pretty happy. He was just wreathing in discomfort for some reason.

Amari narrows her eyes in a glare. "Yeah. I know that. I don't want you, anyway."

"Then why'd you, do it?" Allah presses.

"Do what?"

"Mark me."

Amari winces and furrows her brows in confusion.

"You know, Amari." Allah thrusts Amari back and presses her back against the wall. "I can play this game of yours, but you're not playing fair. I have to walk around with a mate mark on my neck and you get to go mark free. How do you think that makes me feel?"

"What are you talking about? I don't see a mark."

"I asked Amy and my other omegas to use their makeup to cover it up." Allah shakes his head. "Because I can't just waltz in here with *your* mark. Or anywhere else for that matter!"

"Show me."

Allah gets in Amari's face as he snaps. "I'm not walking out of here with it uncovered, Mare!"

Amari winces and that's when Allah realizes what he just called her. Fuck… He can't be calling her that! It shows he cares! Allah can't let Amari know how he truly feels about her!

"Show me. The mark." Amari orders lowly.

Ragnar wants to listen to Amari, but Allah doesn't. *No, don't!* Allah warns Ragnar. But it's too late.

Ragnar moves Allah to rip Amari's black tank top in half at the seams, then rip a piece off to rub off the concealer on his neck. Amari gasps and glares at Allah for his action and he's truly apologetic. He didn't want to do it. But Ragnar had to have his way.

"I'm sorry," Allah mutters. "It's Ragnar."

"Get him." Amari snaps lowly, getting in Allah's space and pressing her breasts into his rib cage, her breasts in a gray sports bra. "Under control!" She orders. She doesn't sound too thrilled for being undressed.

"Yes, ma'am." Allah takes a step back, being submissive for once. This isn't him! What's gotten into him?! Allah is usually dominant towards others. Pushing people to their limits and barking orders. He's a king that's persistent in the safety of others and Hallam's well-being even though he's not its god. Allah gets things done and he's charming when he wants to be.

He has a dominant personality and being submissive is never an option for him. So, being submissive towards someone is new to him. And he has to be submissive with Amari?! He's not in love with her! Yet, for some reason, Ragnar wants to listen and obey her. Let her take over and bark orders at him. Ragnar whines in Allah's head.

*Way to go, Ragnar,* Allah snaps, talking to his wolf. *You just got us in trouble.*

*I'm sorry,* Ragnar responds. *She's just… So perfect. I've got to claim her!*

*Shut up, Ragnar! Or we'll be punished for what you just did!*

*I… I can't help it. I have to have her!*

*What are you, in love? This is not like you! It's not like us!* Allah tries to convince his wolf.

Ragnar continues to whine in Allah's head as if he's in trouble. And in pain. Was he okay? Amari takes the piece of her torn shirt in Allah's hand and wipes away the concealer on his neck, her breath almost tickling his neck. She's so close to him he could just take her in his arms and lay her down on her desk, thrusting into her as they made passionate sex.

There he goes, again! Bad, Allah! Stay focused! Amari stares at the mate mark that's now visible to the naked eye. Anyone would know the golden wings are her touch and no one else's.

"Allah, I'm so," Amari starts, staring at the mate mark that she didn't mean to leave. She cuts herself off and trails off. "I'm so sorry," she finally whispers after a moment of silence. She takes a step back from Allah and presses her back into her bookshelf that Allah left a hole in.

She feels bad. And she should. She just marked Allah! Amari shakes her head. "I didn't mean to… I didn't do it on purpose." She looks up at him. "I swear, Allah. I would *never* do this on purpose. I don't want you. I have Garrett."

"Yeah, well." Allah takes the one step towards Amari and towers over her. "I don't want you either, but Ragnar does. And what he wants, he usually gets."

"Please, forgive me, Allah. I'll make it up to you. In any way. Just tell me what you want and you'll get it."

"An expansion."

Amari winces. He's bringing this up at a time like this? What's wrong with him? Amari has enough on her plate, yet Allah wants to bring it up.

"Amari, it's for the good of the world."

"The world? Or your kingdom?" Amari mumbles.

Allah winces. He can't believe Amari would think of him that way! "Is that how you think of me? Amari? I'm selfish? After all my threats towards you for touching my *wife*."

"Ex-wife."

"Whatever! I think about what's good for Hallam and you think I want it for myself and my kingdom?! You know me!"

"It's what you want, isn't it? More land to call yours."

Allah glares at Amari. "Fuck, no! Now, if you don't mind." Allah takes a step away from Amari, watching her. "I'm taking my wife back to my kingdom."

"She's a warrior, Allah."

Allah winces.

"She's protecting a village on one of the borders. You can forget it."

Allah's heart screams to protect the love of his life and mate. She can't go! She needs to stay where it's safe! A few knocks sound on the office door and Amari quickly walks over to where her desk should be and opens a drawer as it stays hidden. She quickly gets a tank top on then orders for the intruder to come in.

"Amari," Ada says as she comes in.

Allah looks at her and their eyes meet. Her eyes go directly to his mate mark and he instantly feels guilty, his heart breaking. Ada looks at Amari as if she didn't see anything out of the ordinary. Oh, she looks so beautiful. Ada's blue green gaze look past Allah like he's not there. She doesn't acknowledge him in any way.

"The guards are outside waiting for instruction and everyone has evacuated." Ada shakes her head and Allah's heart breaks as he catches a glance of a new mate mark on her neck, tears in his eyes.

Keep it together, Allah! You don't want anyone to know your weakness!

"Thank you, Ada," Amari replies. She walks over to Ada and kisses her cheek. "You're the best second in command."

Ada nods her head. She's what, now?! No! She couldn't betray Allah like that!

"I need you to heal the damage Allah has done to my bookshelf."

"Of course."

"And then make sure no one sees his mate mark. We don't want a riot."

Ada nods her head. "Got it."

Amari holds Ada's wrists and they look into each other's eyes. "I'll give you two a moment."

"That's not necessary."

"But it is." Amari looks back at Allah. "You only got a few minutes with her before she has to get back to it. Make it count."

Allah nods his head and he waits until Amari has walked out of her office and closed the door behind her. He watches Ada, the nineteen-year-old he watched grow up and fall in love with. Oh, he remembers the days very well, spending time with her before she started showing signs of being queer.

Ada holds onto her elbow and looks down, clearly uncomfortable with Allah.

"Ada, I…" Allah starts. He gets cut off as Ada glares at him. He knows that look. Selena used to give it to him all the time whenever he messed up.

"I don't want to hear it from you, Allah," Ada threatens lowly. "You found your second chance mate as if I meant nothing to you. And you know what? I'm glad I never did!"

"But you did. You do! Ada! I'm in love with you!"

"Yeah, well, I've never been in love with *you*." Ada barks, her glare dangerous.

Allah winces at Ada's harshness.

"And I want nothing to do with you! So, after I take care of you, I suggest you move your kingdom and stay as far away as you can from here! I can't believe your second chance mate is my one and only Amari! My queen! My goddess! My everything! And then *my* second chance mate! Your mark was on *her* until I erased it with my own!"

"Wait. What?" Ada's mate had Allah's mate mark? What is he forgetting? Was it May? No… It couldn't be her! She was straight!

"Stay the fuck away from here, Allah. You're not welcome."

"Ada, I'm not leaving without you. I wanna ensure your safety."

"I'm safe here!"

"No." Allah shakes his head as he watches the woman in front him, who is trying to leave Amari's office. "Ada. You're not. You haven't trained in two years. Let me take you back to my kingdom. This is a suicide mission."

Ada snaps and stalks towards Allah. She gets in his face for the very first time and the smell of honeysuckle fills his nostrils. Allah breathes in Ada's scent for the second time, but it doesn't please him like it used to.

Instead, it breaks his heart and makes him yearn for Ada's forgiveness.

"I've trained my whole entire life," Ada hisses. "*Including* these past two years." She spats. She shakes her head. "Amari doesn't make us sitting ducks waiting to be shot down. I've trained even *harder* these past two years and I can finally say that I can take you on in a head-to-head combat."

"Ada. Please. This is nonsense. Come back with me."

Ada pulls her head back and laughs at Allah, her blue-green eyes shining in the dim light of Amari's lamp. "And do what? Your maids? Your three omegas that are bisexual and doing it with each other behind your back."

"I rejected them two years ago, Ada. After finding out what they were doing."

"Yeah, that's your problem! You're strictly straight and don't allow the ell, gee, bee, tee, queue into your kingdom. You're going to Hell's Fire for this."

Allah winces at Ada's threat. She's brave to talk to him like this! He narrows his eyes at her. "What's gotten into you? You were never like this before." Allah remembers a time Ada was submissive.

"Amari and May. It's amazing what the right people influence you to do. Be yourself and stand up for what you believe in." Ada turns her back to Allah and starts for the door.

"My door will always be open. Ada. For you. Cause I'll always love you. And welcome you back."

Ada looks back at her shoulder, her eyes hiding behind it and not letting Allah see her facial expression.

"I'll never come back." She threatens with a growl. Ada walks out of Amari's office and that's when Allah remembers. She was supposed to take care of a couple things!

Allah looks at the bookshelf he punched a hole in to find it repaired with the magic spell intact. His hand goes straight to his neck and he feels his mate mark. But the question is… Can you see it?

Allah walks over to a mirror on a wall and he notices his mate mark is missing. The naked eye can't see it, but he can feel it.

"Oh," Ada pipes up as she peeks in.

Allah looks at her through the mirror and their eyes meet.

"Amari was just toying with you earlier. She didn't have a quickie with my mate and I. It just hurt for you because you decided to mark my mate when she was your rival's soon-to-be Luna. She got rejected because of it. Remember that?" Ada closes the door behind her before Allah can reply, leaving him in the silence of Amari's big office.

Guilt hits him like a freight train and he instantly regrets putting Amari through the pain. He did it all for nothing! How could he be so stupid?! Allah needs to apologize to Amari once she gets a moment.

And who knew when that would be!

# 10

Amari looks at Garrett as he waits for her word, talking to her guards, housekeeper, and butler. Garrett is Amari's commander, in charge of security at her estate. But with code nine they have to make it look like the estate has been abandoned. Not a soul can be spotted here.

The only problem is the hellhounds. They'll come rummaging through everything if security doesn't keep an eye on them.

"Garrett," Amari starts. "I want you to coordinate with your team with keeping the hellhounds at bay. Without a goddess and security team in Hell's Fire they're roaming around and getting out of hand."

Garrett nods his head at Amari and she continues to roam her eyes around everyone.

"I want you all to stay safe. And out of sight. If Kera sees any of you here, she'll know the estate hasn't been abandoned. Best plan of attack for that is to look like that your homeless and just looking for shelter. Make it look natural. Don't try too hard or she'll know something is up. Kera is smart. She'll be coming here to challenge me and threaten Mike's life. I'm not going to be here. I'm going to be where she least expects me to be."

"And where's that," Baron asks. "Cause there's a few places I can think of." He teases.

Amari laughs teasingly but sarcastically. "King Allah's kingdom. He and I rarely get along, but it's Madi he hates most. He doesn't like that she's becoming the goddess of Hell's Fire and would prefer if it was ruled by me while Viggo takes the throne as God of Hallam. We're gonna let Kera think that's the plan."

"But you've been officiated as the heir to Hallam. Not Hell's Fire."

"There's a way for Kera to think the other way around. Ada and Amelia are working on that."

"Amelia?" Whispers of speculation travel through the men and women of security.

Amari nods her head, knowing why. "Yes. I know she's done horrible things in the past. But she was trying to do it for the good of Hallam. She deserves the benefit of the doubt."

Baron nods his head in understanding. "Understood." He mumbles.

Garrett looks at his men and women. "Alright, ladies and gentleman. You know what to do. Let's agree on who gets to be homeless first."

The men and women chuckle as Garrett watches them admirably. They're the best in what they do and they're like family. Garrett can't stand the thought of any of them getting hurt or killed. If Kera tries to go after his men and women, he'll be the one to put a bullet in her head. Bullseye style.

Garrett couldn't lose his family. Nor his girlfriend he so loved.

∞

Amari turns towards her estate and she starts for the back, taking a shortcut through her home. Henry joins her side.

"They're not joining us anytime soon," Henry puts in, referring to the creatures of his kind that live in forests throughout Hallam.

"Of course, not," Amari replies. "They're phoenixes." She looks at her butler. "They'll come around when necessary."

Henry nods his head. "Are you really going to go with King Allah?"

"It's my only option, Henry. I've got to go." Amari feels a presence at the door of her estate. She looks over there to see Allah. He hasn't left? "Besides. I'll be safe there until I'm crowned. But it doesn't stop me from going out and looking for Mike. I think I prefer to find him first anyway."

Henry nods his head as Amari looks at him. "I'll send word to Viggo." He speaks up.

"He's the best sailor we've got." Amari mentions. "And Viking. I want him ready when I leave. But that won't be for a couple days. I got some matters to attend to first."

"Of course." Henry pulls away and Klauss joins Amari.

"Are you sure this is the right choice," Klauss mumbles next to her, not wanting anyone to overhear. "You know what he'll do."

"He's not going to do anything without my consent," Amari mutters.

"That's not what I'm worried about."

Amari stops and faces her best friend, knowing where he's going with this. "It won't happen again, Klauss."

"How can you be so sure? Plus… You have all of Ada's eggs. And he wants kids with her!"

"And I plan on derailing his plan."

"Amari… I know you."

"And I know Allah. He'll try to get me pregnant, yes. But I got the best birth control."

"I heard it's an I-U-D! That's not the best!"

"I've never gotten pregnant, now, have I?" Amari defends herself.

Klauss sighs and sags. "No," he mumbles after a moment. "But I still don't want him anywhere near you. He'll seduce you!"

"If he tries, I'll kill him."

Klauss clenches his jaw. "Fine. But I'm coming with."

"You don't like wolves, Klauss."

"I'm willing to put up with them for you."

Amari sets her hand on Klauss's cheek lovingly. She loves this man as her brother and best friend. He's always been there for her in her dreams. "I prefer you go back home and have your men look for Kera there. Unless I decide to get crowned under the radar, there's no point in you being here."

Klauss nods his head briefly. "Understood."

Amari gets grabbed and turned around. She looks up in time before Garrett's lips crash on hers. She wraps her arms around his neck and traps his lips against hers, not wanting him to pull away from her.

"I fear this may be the last time I see you," Garrett says roughly into Amari's lips. He holds onto her, keeping her close to him.

She rests her forehead on his chin. "Me too." Amari closes her eyes. "I don't want you to go."

Garrett brushes Amari's temple with the back of his fingers then lifts her chin, making their eyes meet. "You'll find my nephew. I know you will."

"It's a shame you can't come with."

Garrett presses his lips into Amari's forehead. He holds onto her tightly. Oh… The things he's done for her. She's afraid to lose her commander. Her chief. Her beloved… Her new best friend.

"I love you," Garrett whispers into Amari's forehead, his hand holding the back of her neck softly. "And I always have."

"I love you, too." Amari tightens her grip on Garrett, not wanting him to go. "And please… Be safe."

Garrett rests his forehead on Amari's forehead. He caresses her jaw with his thumb.

"I'll find you."

"Not before I find you." Garrett says roughly with a soft tone.

Amari opens her mouth and tastes Garrett's cologne. It's strong. But it smells like him. Cedarwood mixes with fresh ocean air and Amari finds herself drawn to it more than ever. She grabs the collar of Garrett's black t-shirt and she pulls him into her.

Their lips clash together. It isn't long before their tongues clash, sparring and stroking each other. Amari so wishes she has time to take Garrett to the bedroom. But she has to go. He has to go! Garrett's free hand rubs Amari's waist, letting her know he's wanting the same thing as her. But their tongues continue to clash, spar, and stroke each other. They get heated from the touch.

Amari gets reminded why she does this. Protect what she loves. And she can't wait to rule Hallam with Garrett beside her. She hopes this isn't the last time she sees him. She prays to her Father above while she makes out with the new love of her life, moving on completely from Mike. She asks Him to keep Garrett and his men and women safe and protected. She asks for a safe passage to find Mike.

Amari doesn't leave anything out in her prayer and soon Garrett is finally moving his lips away from hers, taking a breath. She misses them right away. Garrett rests his forehead on Amari's forehead in silence then steps back, walking away until she can't feel him anymore. Amari shudders a sigh. She opens her eyes just for them to meet his back. Her heart aches for his touch and closeness, breaking at the thought that she possibly won't ever, again.

∞

Allah hangs back, watching Amari and Garrett as they say goodbye. What they have is most definitely just as strong as what Allah had with Selena.

He gets reminded of his first wife. The first woman he ever loved and married. Sure, he loved girls when he was a kid and teenager. But it wasn't until Selena that he found true love.

Selena's dark hair brought out her fair skin and complexion. Her purple eyes were unique and their son had them. Allah would do anything to look into those purple eyes once more and tell his first wife and son that he missed them. Allah wants to be a family, again. He so misses the connection that he had with Selena. He thought he had it with Ada, but she wants nothing to do with him.

Allah was selfless with Selena. She brought out the best in him and helped him become the king that he is, now. Because of Selena, Allah is more caring. And forgiving. He was dominant with her, but careful. He knew just the right buttons to push to get her to relax and tell him about her day. And she had the most care-free attitude that changed into a very loving wife, mother, and friend that made Allah marry her.

His heart breaking for Amari he starts for her, knowing how she feels. This is how Allah felt before every battle. He had no idea if he would see Selena, again. Allah stops just after taking a few steps towards Amari as he started to reconsider. If he wrapped his arms around her… How would that look in front of her people that she cares about most?

To her, Allah is just a great king and God. They've *never* been friends! He's just her mentor! Allah hangs back and waits for Amari to come to him. She takes another moment to herself, Klauss wrapping his arm around her and comforting her.

It's best that Klauss does that. It would look bad for Allah if he were to step in. Klauss and Amari take a moment together. They start laughing, Amari laughing through her tears. Allah heightens his hearing to listen to their conversation.

"Yeah, I don't think Adeline would really like that," Amari says softly. "I mean…"

"She's not the type to just let it slide," Klauss puts in.

"No," Amari drags out. "I'm not going to kiss you. And for many reasons, too."

Klauss nods his head. "Come on," he whispers in Amari's ear.

Allah watches Klauss and Amari in the moonlight as they hug. He spots Klauss's hand holding onto Amari's forearm gently.

"Let's deal with this idiot."

"You know he can probably hear you," Amari mumbles. "At least… If he's using his lycan hearing."

"Well, then he should know that I know about your quarrels earlier today. *Both*. Of them."

"He punched a hole in the wall." Amari speaks lowly.

Allah growls at the news. She *told* him? Her best friend! How is Allah going to get Amari alone, now! Since

Klauss knows what went down in Ada's bedroom, the forest, and now Amari's office Allah may *never* get Amari alone!

Klauss and Amari start for Allah and he hangs back. He cuts off the heightened hearing and lets it go back to normal. When Klauss and Amari reach Allah they look at each other. The look on his face must reveal that he knows.

Amari looks up at Allah. "Since you're still here," Amari starts. "I'm coming with you. To your kingdom."

"Are you sure your boyfriend here is going to let you," Allah asks, his arms crossed against his chest, guarded.

Klauss snorts and Allah glares at him. Klauss holds back a smirk, showing some sort of inside joke. Allah furrows his brows as he deepens his glare.

"*Klauss* is okay with it," Amari corrects Allah. "It's just your attitude that's the problem."

Allah dips his head to Klauss in respect as he remembers. "Your majesty. I'm so sorry about your father. He was a great king."

"Thank you," Klauss replies softly. He looks at Amari. "I'll see you soon."

Amari nods her head at Klauss. He lets his hand land on her lower back before walking away. She looks up at Allah.

"Can we go?" She whispers softly.

"Yeah," Allah drags out with softness. He takes a few steps back and shifts, letting Ragnar take over.

*Whatever you do. Don't piss her off.* Allah warns Ragnar.

Ragnar nods his head briefly then lies down to let Amari climb onto his back. She uses his elbow as leverage then swings her leg around him, settling her legs on his back. Ragnar stands up and he feels a pull towards a creature that's deep inside Amari. He can hear it scratching and gasping for air.

Ragnar reaches out to Amari's creature deep inside of her. But it lashes out at him angrily and defensively. He quickly pulls out and flinches. He shakes his head and his fur around his neck shakes. Amari pets Ragnar's fur.

"You okay," Amari asks Ragnar in a soft tone.

He looks back at her and gives her a small nod, winking at her with a smile on his face.

"Then let's go."

Ragnar sprints forward and a few seconds later he's jumping over a hedge lining the property, into the field next to Amari's estate. He races for the lycan kingdom and feels the wind in his fur. Amari grasps onto some strands of his fur to stay on his back. She leans forward, her breath on his ear.

Having no idea what she's doing to him, he pushes forward as he's able to go faster with her help.

Her scent of lavender and vanilla washes over Ragnar and it gets to Allah, who goes crazy for the scent to stop taking its effect on him.

*You really don't like it, do you,* Ragnar asks.

*It's not that,* Allah replies. *She just made her decision. And I've made mine.*

Ragnar shakes his head at Allah. *Your loss.*

Allah goes quiet and lets Ragnar race in silence, pushing on his speed and covering ten miles in just twenty minutes. When he enters the walls of his kingdom he slows down. He stops at the path that leads to the castle's entrance. The castle stands tall in the moonlight, reflecting the light of the moon. Amari sits up straight as Ragnar starts forward in a walk.

"Oh. Wow." Amari breathes.

Ragnar takes his time, letting Amari take in the sights. She's never seen a castle in real life before and Allah's castle is no ordinary castle. In the light of a full moon, the silver castle glows and radiates a protective light that guides the lost, calling to them by name.

Ragnar passes the hedges that line out the courtyard in front of the castle. The fountain in the middle has four wolf heads howling at the moon while the water gently gushes out above them and cascades around them.

The four wolves represent the four lycan kings that came together at the great battle with Kera and helped put her in the prisons of Hell's Fire. The lights on the fountain glow bright and show off spouts shooting out water underneath the wolves' heads and into a big round bath. Underneath it is a much bigger bath with juvenile koi fish.

Ragnar dips his head as he makes it to the water fountain. He looks down at the fish. Some look like they're ready to be moved to the six-acre pond that marks the south border of the Asgard Lycan pack and the Blue Moon werewolf pack.

Amari leans over and grabs the head of the first Asgard Lycan King. Ragnar stops and looks back at her as she gently smooths her hand over the features of the howling wolf. Does she know that's Ragnar? He can hear Amari's heart calm down as her hand traces over the top of the head and towards the ears. What is she thinking? Allah so wishes he could get inside of Amari's head. But the mind link would be prodding her mind and she'd be aware of Allah's attempt.

Amari swings her leg over, sitting on Ragnar like a princess or a queen on a horse. But she turns her body towards the fountain and trails both of her hands over the head of Ragnar on the fountain. Her fingers trace every hair on the head and they fall down to the front of the neck. Ragnar would love for Amari to run her fingers through his fur and give him that spark of energy to make him run faster. Her delicate fingers that are now tracing every single inch of the muzzle on the statue. Allah is able to slip into Amari's unexpected mind with no detection.

*That's my wolf,* Allah mutters in the mind link.

Amari pulls her hands off of the statue and puts them on her thighs. She clears throat and looks at Ragnar. His gold eyes meet her brown eyes. "Right, then."

Ragnar carries forward in silence and Amari holds onto his fur, tucking her legs in underneath her. He walks over to the entrance of the castle and stops a few paces away. He looks back at Amari. She instantly looks tired. She slides off of his back and starts forward.

Ragnar shifts instantly and lets Allah take over. Allah quickly grabs the gym shorts in the hedge right next to him and puts them on. Then he strides over to Amari and sweeps her off of her feet with one motion, carrying her bridal style and never missing a step.

"Allah, I can walk," Amari mumbles, her voice sounding tired.

"You're tired," Allah replies. "You've had a long day. Let me take care of you."

Amari looks at Allah as his butler opens the door to let them in, knowing via mind link. "*You've.* Had a long day." Amari retorts.

Allah looks at his butler. "Thank you, Maverik."

"My pleasure," Maverik replies. "Does the lady need any clothes to change into?"

Allah looks at Amari and their eyes meet, her arms around his neck. "No." He looks at his butler. "We're good. Thank you."

"Don't listen to him," Amari speaks up. Maverik looks at her. "I would love a nighty at least. And in the morning, I would love a dress. The maids can choose the color for me."

"Of course, Queen Amari." Maverik dips his head then closes the door.

"Thank you," Amari calls softly as Maverik walks away.

He acknowledges her with a wave of his hand and disappears to find the maids. Allah starts for his quarters in the west wing, but Amari stops him.

"No," Amari drags out. "Mm, mmm."

Allah looks at Amari. "What?"

"I want my own wing. I'm not staying in your quarters."

"Amari."

"No!" Amari orders. "I am not your wife! Put me down and I'll find my way to the east wing."

"Not happening." Allah starts for the west wing and Amari quickly pushes herself out of his arms, finding her footing gracefully.

"This isn't my first rodeo, Allah. And in fact. It won't be my last."

Allah holds back a growl, not wanting to give Amari the satisfaction of knowing she's pushing his buttons. Again.

"I'm staying in the east wing."

Allah sighs in frustration. "Amari, come on."

"Do you wanna give the wrong impression?"

Should he tell her? That everybody in the castle already knew she's his second chance mate? Allah thinks about it for a quick moment, making the thought look like hesitance. "No."

"Then I'm going to the east wing." Amari turns and starts for the opposite direction, where the east wing is.

"They already know."

Amari stops dead in her tracks, her back to Allah. She doesn't turn around.

"Everybody in the castle. They know you're my second chance mate thanks to your *stupid* mistake." Allah spats the word 'stupid', keeping his eyes on Amari's back. He's not quite excited for what she did to him. But he still cared for her. "You're lucky they can keep a secret."

"Well, Ada's magic spell on your mark won't fade or break as long as you continue to wish to keep it hidden. And lucky for me you didn't mark me. So, I'm safe."

"I'd like to change that, by the way." Allah starts for Amari, walking slowly towards her. "I'd like for you to suffer the same way I am."

"Not gonna happen."

"Really." It's a question. Allah crosses his arms as he stands right behind Amari and he notices her body tensing up. Does she really hate him that much? "Cause it's only fair for us both to, you know… Suffer the consequences."

Amari looks to her side and hides her eyes behind her shoulder, barely peeking them over. What is it with Allah's women tonight?! "Too bad you have Klauss, Garrett, Adam, Viggo, and the whole entire world to get through first."

"I'll take my chances," Allah says lowly, actually daring to take on two takals. One of which is a Viking and the Viking takals are tougher than most!

They can kill you with just a flick of their wrist.

"Good luck," Amari challenges in a soothing tone. "Cause you're gonna need it." She walks away from Allah and leaves him standing there in front of the staircase for the west wing, looking stupid.

## <u>11</u>

Amari wakes up to a few women in the bedroom, whispering excitedly about the dress they brought for her. She groggily opens her eyes halfway and she watches the three omegas at work.

There's two brunettes and a woman with raven black hair. One brunette is dressed in a maroon maid's dress with a cream-colored apron. The other brunette is in a dark green maid's dress with a white apron. Both dresses have lace on them in the dresses same color.

"I'm going to fix the petticoat really quick," the woman with raven black hair whispers. "It has a tear in a seam."

"Can you get a different slip," the brunette in maroon whispers. "This one is trash."

The first woman gasps quietly, walking over to the one in maroon. "Already?"

The first brunette holds the slip up to show a grease stain.

"How did that get past my inspection?"

"King Allah. I smell him all over these clothes."

"King Allah can kiss my ass." The raven black haired woman snatches the slip from the brunette in maroon.

"Join the club," Amari mumbles, sitting up in the bed. She groans and puts her forehead in her palm, already feeling a headache coming on.

"Queen Amari," the first woman speaks up. "I'm so sorry if we woke you." That voice… It sounds so familiar.

"No. Not at all." Amari takes a deep breath as she lifts her head, her eyes closed. She looks at the raven black haired omega. "Do you guys have any aspirin? My head is killing me."

"Yes, of course."

The brunette in green walks into the bathroom and a moment later she comes back with a glass of water and two white pills in her palm.

"We had the perfect dress picked out for you. But it seems King Allah decided to destroy it."

Amari looks at the maid that brings her the glass of water and pills. "Thank you." She looks at the raven black haired woman and that's when she finally recognizes the woman.

She's not a maid whatsoever! Amari chokes on the water as she takes the pills. She sets the glass down. "Sirena! Oh my god!" Amari jumps out of bed and runs over to her cousin she lost a few years ago in a car accident. She was killed by a drunk driver.

Amari and Sirena hug, clinging onto each other. She can't believe her eyes! Sirena made it into Hallam! She must have chosen to come here to prolong her life! Happy tears fill Amari's eyes and she holds onto the back of Sirena's head.

They cling onto each other, happy to be reunited. They were so close! Sirena comes from Amari's dad's side of the family. Madi comes from Amari's mom's side of the family. Amari and Sirena were inseparable, stuck to each other's hips like glue. They were sisters. And they never done anything without the other.

At the same age as each other, they went to the same school and had the same circle of friends. Sirena's boyfriend in high school was an ass. But after college he came back a different man and proposed to her with a big diamond. They got married not long after. And on their way home from their honeymoon a drunk driver hit them in a head-on, killing both of them instantly.

The tears in Amari's eyes finally fall as Sirena squeezes her tightly, saying those three words that always does her in.

"Missed you, bestie," Sirena whispers into Amari's shoulder.

"Yeah," Amari manages out, her throat tight. "I missed you, too."

Sirena moans as her hold finally starts to loosen a little.

Her face falls into Amari's shoulder and they stay like that for a moment longer. They pull away from each other to look at the other. Sirena moves Amari's bangs out of her face, her fingertips brushing Amari's forehead.

"You never changed a bit," Sirena says softly.

"Neither have you." Amari holds Sirena's cheek in her hand, her eyes soft and full of love.

Sirena traps Amari's hand on her face, pressing her hand into it with comfort and leaning her cheek into it as she closes her eyes. A tear falls down her cheek and meets Amari's thumb who wipes it away.

"Looks like you still got those contacts," Amari breathes.

Sirena looks at Amari, her violet eyes shining bright. "Actually, I was born with these here."

Amari pulls her head back in surprise. "What?" She whispers.

Sirena curls her fingers around Amari's hand and pulls it away from her face just to hold it in her hands. "I died with the contacts in. The moon goddess decided purple fits me better than brown. I mean..." Sirena shrugs. "It's better for a siren anyway."

"Oh my gosh. I love it!" Amari squeals at the thought of her cousin being the first siren here. She hugs her best friend. "You're the first siren!"

"I know!" Sirena's arms wrap around Amari's torso and her hands settle on Amari's shoulders. "I'm excited with this change. And it's been great living here with these two lovely women."

Amari turns to the two brunettes, finding out that they're identical twins. "Hello! Please, tell me your names."

"I'm Amy," the one in maroon says. She shakes Amari's hand in a firm grip and shake.

"Amy." Realization hits Amari. This is Allah's favorite maid! How did Amari manage to get her?

"And I'm Lexi," the one in green speaks up.

Amari turns and shakes Lexi's hand. For some reason Lexi is the least liked in the Lycan kingdom. There's nothing wrong with her and she's absolutely beautiful. As a matter of fact, Lexi just married a man that courted her for almost ten years. She is now Allah's Beta's wife.

"Lexi," Amari drags out. "Congratulations. Again."

"Thank you." Lexi sets her free hand over her and Amari's shaking hands, stopping the motion and settling her blue eyes on Amari's brown eyes. "That was quite the pleasure. Seeing you for a few moments. You were in and out."

"Restless night. I couldn't sleep very well."

"That's okay. Everybody still doesn't believe that you were there. They think I was just hallucinating."

"Well, I haven't really had any dreams in the past two weeks thanks to work. Henry told me everybody was starting to get really worried."

"I tried to reassure them, but. Like I said."

Amari nods her head and turns to Amy. "Now, how did I score you? You're Allah's favorite."

Amy shrugs. "I snuck away undetected."

"There's no hard feelings, are there? I mean... I know you're an omega here. But..."

Amy shakes her head, interrupting Amari. "I used to warm his bed all the time after Selena passed. But then Ada came..." Amy trails off and rubs her upper arm as she holds Amari's soft stare. "And then he just wanted to get back at you last night."

"That actually wasn't me." Amari mutters.

Amy's eyes light up with shock and confusion. She looks at Sirena for a moment then back at Amari. "It wasn't?"

Amari shakes her head.

"But how?"

"May. Remember her role in the Asgard Light Moon pack?"

"Oh, my goddess." Amy's hand flies to her mouth in shock.

"Well, let's just say her second chance mate is his soon-to-be ex-wife and she gave Ada the release she needed from the pain."

"Yesterday was quite eventful, then."

"It sure was." Amari squeezes Amy's hand that's next to her side. "Now. If Allah is gonna throw a tantrum over me being in the east wing, let's get me into something that's going to steal his breath. We don't wanna take it away. We wanna snatch it and never give it back."

Amy smirks. "I know just the dress."

"Yes!" Lexi exclaims.

Amari looks at Lexi as she jumps and claps her hands excitedly. Lexi brings herself back together and stands still. She clears her throat.

"Sorry." She looks down at the floor for a moment. "It's just a dress that was Selena's that made all the wolves and Lycan's want her," Lexi manages out as she looks at Amari and their eyes meet. "It's a shame that they all left her behind when she needed them most."

"Yeah," Amy drags out. "Where's the loyalty?" She snaps.

"Gone," Amari replies. "Loyalty towards women is gone. It's all for the men, now."

"Yeah, I'd like to change that," Amy remarks as she sticks her hip out and puts her hand on it. She truly is a woman of good stature and modesty. She's never been one to seek out revenge from what Amari remembers.

Amari smirks. "Let's start that change. Shall we?"

Amy smiles to show off her canines, vengeance clearly on her mind. "We shall."

∞

Amari puts her hand to her bodice as Sirena pulls a string through a hole of the corset that goes with Selena's black dress.

It's very low cut and has a country feel to it with the black lace all over the tube top that fits perfectly around the breasts with its round shape above the breasts and the lace continues all the way down the skirt. The black lace turns silver at the top of the tube top and continues up on the sides. It turns into sleeves around the shoulders and down the arms. It continues over the wrists and there's two perfect notches in the lace to stick your thumbs and fingers through, the sleeves turning into half-gloves.

The dress is absolutely phenomenal. For some reason the dress reminds Amari of Garrett and she instantly misses him.

"What did Selena wear this dress to," Amari asks Sirena.

"Uh," Sirena drawls out.

*A funeral*, Selena replies to Amari. *My father's. And then I wore it whenever I thought of him. I had one just like it when I was a little girl and it was his favorite dress.*

*Selena, I…* Amari feels guilty for wearing the dress, hoping there was another option.

*No. Don't feel guilty. My father was Garrett's father back in Homba. The dress belongs to you, now.*

Amari nods her head then looks back at Sirena. "Never mind. Selena just responded."

Sirena looks at Amari.

"She wore it to her father's funeral who was Garrett's father back in Homba. She wore it whenever she missed him after that."

"Oh my gosh," Sirena breathes, moved by the comment so much there's tears in her eyes. "I didn't…"

"Not very many people know." Amari looks down in front of herself as she starts to remember. "Including lycans."

"It's so cool you can converse with her, though. I've never heard of anyone that can do that. Not even Allah can do it!"

Amari looks back at Sirena. "It's a special gift."

"Do you think I could do it?"

"If you practiced your magic every day."

Sirena nods her head. "Alright. Suck your stomach in."

Amari looks ahead and grabs onto the bed frame canopy post. Sirena shifts and Amari knows she's looking over her shoulder and at her face.

"You might wanna hold onto something stronger than that."

"I volunteer," Amy screams from the bathroom. "I volunteer!" She runs into the bedroom and looks at Amari. Their eyes meet and Amy puts on her best Katniss Everdeen act. "I volunteer as tribute."

Amari laughs full-heartedly. She had no idea! "Does Allah know?"

Amy shakes her head. "After he found out about the two, I decided to stay quiet."

"I know lesbians are usually the ones that only have it. But… Do you?"

Amy shakes her head. "I have the full set."

Amari winces. "Wait… What?"

"Amy," Sirena starts. "Less chit chat, more pulling. She's going to be late for lunch. She's already missed breakfast by sleeping in."

Amy walks over to Amari and offers her two hands. Amari looks at them a little hesitantly for once. A she-man! Now, that's even rarer! Amari looks at Amy.

"You're not," Amari starts. "A lycan. Are you?"

"I'm part lycan and part merman."

"So… The mermaid in you comes from your mom." Amari points at Amy.

"Amari," Sirena interrupts. "Just take her hands, please."

"Oh. Right." Amari pushes past the awkwardness and takes Amy's hand, who braces herself.

"Actually, it comes from my dad," Amy replies. "Pretty ironic, isn't it?"

"But it's the mermaids that get to choose."

Amy nods her head. "I was born a mermaid and got to choose when the time came. But I couldn't make a decision since I like both men and women. So..." Amy drags 'so' out. "I got both."

Sirena yanks the corset tighter unexpectedly and Amari gasps at the tightness as Amy keeps her from falling back. For some reason she gets awakened down there. She usually doesn't know what to think about a literal she-man! They got the breasts up top and then the penis and testicles underneath. They usually don't have a vagina as well, though! So, this is new to Amari and it's why she can't wrap her head around it.

"How could you get both," Amari asks. "I mean... Does your clitoris turn into... A penis?"

"Yes and no."

Amari looks at Amy in confusion and their eyes meet. Amy shrugs.

"It's hard to explain."

"Then show me."

"Okay," Sirena drawls out after tying the strings and securing the corset. Amari stands up straight and watches Sirena as she throws her hands up and starts for the door. She looks at Amari and Amy as she puts her hand on the door knob. "I'll let you two lovebirds finish it up."

Amari snorts and presses her lips together. Oh, how wrong Sirena is! Amari could *never* think that way about Amy! Allah would *definitely* kill her if she did! But yet there she goes. Sirena walks out of the bedroom and Amari looks at Amy. Amy nods her head at Amari with her eyes in slits.

"Sirena can sever the mate bond for a moment so you can get a full taste without Allah getting suspicious," Amy says, replying to a question in Amari's head that she had no idea she had.

"Can she really do that," Amari asks.

"Of course!"

Sirena walks into the bedroom a moment later. "This is going to be so weird," she says in a tone of disbelief as she shakes her head. She starts for Amari. "Amari, I'm so sorry for this. Amy…" She looks at Amy. "You owe me for this." Sirena pushes Amari's hair back and her lips instantly land on the mate mark spot on Amari's neck.

Amari widens her eyes in surprise as Sirena sinks her canines into her flesh. Sirena creates a temporary mate mark there. Sirena breathes on it with her magic and then a moment later she's out of the bedroom.

Amari looks at Amy in shock.

"Don't worry," Amy says. "It'll fade by time we're done."

Amari takes a step towards Amy. "Just so you know… I don't do one-night stands. We do it and you're one of my mistresses. There won't be going back."

Amy starts picking up her skirts. "I'll move in with you after the war is over. And so will my sister and Sirena."

"Lexi chose to be female, though."

Amy nods her head. "Yes. That's correct. Though sometimes I wonder if she should've chosen to be a male," she mumbles, looking down at the floor.

Amari motions her chin at Amy, looking down there on her. "Show me."

Amy smirks. "Get up and close to get the full effect."

"Yes, ma'am." Amari gets down on her knees right in front of Amy and pokes her head into Amy's skirts.

She pulls Amy's panties down, making the she-man step out of them. Amari lets her breath tickle Amy's clitoris and vulva. Amari starts to suck on Amy's clitoris and makes her gasp. Oh, she loves it when she gets a woman going with just one quick move!

Amy grabs onto the canopy post on the bed, making it shake a little, as Amari starts to eat her out. She licks and sucks on Amy's clitoris and starts to feel a change, Amy's clitoris starting to sink into itself. Amari changes course and thrusts her tongue into Amy's opening. She licks the walls and fucks Amy with her tongue.

The tip of Amari's tongue meets with something with a small hole at the end and she knows it's the tip of Amy's penis. Her penis grows and it glides onto Amari's tongue then into her mouth. Unexpectedly, it grows right down Amari's throat and makes her choke.

"Fuck," Amy drawls out. "That's a first."

Amari chokes on a laugh, a smile on her face and her eyes shift up as if she can see Amy's face while Amy's penis stays deep in her throat. Oh, yeah. Amari knows how to find the weird ones. She's going to have fun with this. Two mistresses are plenty!

Amari starts to suck on Amy's cock and before she knows it, Amy is grasping onto her hair and making her deep throat her cock. Amari has forgotten how massive mermen's cocks are! They fill up a woman's opening all the way, barely leaving any room for a man that may want a three-some.

Amari pulls away for a quick moment. "Amy," she whispers. She licks Amy just above the penis. "I wanna feel you inside of me."

Amy growls. "I would love that, Amari."

Amari stands up and she leads Amy over to the bed. She lays down on her back on the bed, watching Amy. Amy gets in between Amari's thighs, picking up her skirts, and she pushes Amari's panties aside.

Amy guides herself inside of Amari, making Amari throw her head back and have an orgasm with the fullness inside of her.

"Fuck," Amari breathes. She grabs onto the headboard as Amy thrusts into her and she sees pure bliss as she has an intense orgasm with every thrust.

"Amy!"

# 12

Allah reaches across the table to grab a cracker as he reads an interesting article in a newspaper that came from Homba. Well… The story is more tragic than interesting.

Allah pops a Cheez-it cracker into his mouth as he reads the story of a car-wreck on a road called I-89. A car was going southbound when it hit a patch of black ice and caused a train of wrecks behind it. Luckily, nobody was killed. But the man in the car that started the train suffered a migraine and a broken leg.

Allah has never been that interested to try and cross over to Homba. The stories he reads in its newspapers are tragic. Mainly because you hear more about bad news than good news. That world seems to be filled with bad people more than good people! All the ignorance… Allah could *never* live there.

He reaches for more Cheez-it crackers and a female hand smacks his hand away. He glances up to see which female it is then looks at his paper. Sirena. She gets away with anything since Amari is now here in Hallam. Who knows what Amari would do!

"Hey, Sirena. What's going on?" It takes a moment. But when he finally comes around, Allah widens his eyes in shock at his newspaper as he remembers, drinking his glass of water. He spits his water out. Fuck! He forgot to tell Sirena about Amari!

"Sirena," Allah starts in an all-knowingly fear. He puts his paper and water down and stands up, hitting his penis on the underside of the table. He doubles over with his hand on the table as pain shoots through his penis. That hurt!

"King Allah," Sirena says in a nonchalant tone. "You really shouldn't spoil your appetite."

Allah waits the pain out as it takes its time. He stands up once it's gone, looking at Amari's cousin. "Right." He clears his throat. "What can I do for you?"

Sirena points over Allah's shoulder, indicating what's behind him as she looks at the entrance to the dining room. "That."

Allah looks behind himself to find Amari coming into the dining room in the dress Selena loved so much. His heart drops and he instantly knows Amari misses Garrett.

Amy and Lexi follow behind Amari, getting an unexpected growl escaping Allah's throat. How did Amy slip through his fingers? She's not to be around Amari!

Allah has his reasons! Amy is his favorite omega and Amari is about to become a goddess!

Allah can't lose Amy to Amari as a maid! He *won't* lose his best people to her!

"Let it be, Allah," Sirena coos, using her siren magic on him to calm him down. "Just focus on my cousin. Use your time to be with her while she's here."

She stands right behind Allah as he watches Amari walk over and sit on his left. At least Amari knows table etiquette! Sirena mind links with Allah as he sits back down and watches Amari get comfortable in her chair.

*I see Garrett's future by just simply reading my cousin. She agreed to wear that dress after speaking with Selena.*

*You keep my wife out of this, Sirena,* Allah growls in his head threateningly.

Sirena walks over and curls her hand around the top of the open chair next to Amari. *Nevertheless. He's not going to live for much longer. And you* can't *let Amari have the time to choose Viggo over you. Because if she has a moment to choose once asked. You won't like her answer.*

*We can't be together anyway.* Allah glares at Sirena and she meets his glare with a stern look and her chin high.

Amari looks between Allah and Sirena. She instantly knows they're conversing through a mind link, eating a few Cheez-it crackers.

She decides to watch the scene and be patient.

*Yes, you can,* Sirena persists. *Stop being so bullheaded, Allah. She's a perfect Luna and goddess for you!*

Allah grips the end of the table tightly. *Back off, Sirena. I am not going to betray Ada, again. You know this all too well.*

*Ada betrayed you! The moment she ran from you for trying to touch her! We both know this all too well.* Sirena sneers with a smirk on her face.

Allah growls a warning to her.

*Just make her choose you, Allah. Get to know her. Have drinks. Have a laugh. Have sex.*

Allah's grip shifts and he cracks the table. *I will* not *be doing that, again! Amari and I only did it the one time because she wanted to release me from my pain.*

*And look where that got you.*

*Sirena! I'm warning you!* Allah wasn't liking where this conversation was going. And for good reason. He wasn't about to have sex with the woman he trained as a goddess. Not again.

*Growl and bark at me all you want.* Sirena shifts and holds onto her teacup with both hands, her violet eyes baring into Allah's silver-gray eyes. She sticks out her hip as she gives him attitude. *But we both know you can't touch me. Amari would kill you if you did.*

*If you were my mate instead of her!*

*The situation would be completely different and she wouldn't even be here at all.*

Allah's lips part slightly as his glare deepens. Sirena throws her raven black hair back over her shoulder, her head tilted.

*Just give my cousin a chance. And you'll see what I see.*

Allah continues to glare at Sirena, but she cuts off the mind link with ease before he can object to her insane suggestion. Amari clears her throat, noticing the tension.

"Sirena, are you going to eat with us," she asks, knowing it's safe to start up a conversation.

"Allah put me in with the maids," Sirena says plainly. "You two have fun." She starts for the maids' quarters, but she doesn't get very far, stopping at the sound of Amari's hand slamming down on the table.

Fuck. Sirena was waiting for that by the way she sauntered!

"Only until Amari got here," Allah defends himself before Amari can blow up on him. That's a lie.

"Still," Amari snaps. "She is not a maid, Allah! She's a queen!"

Allah looks at Amari, not that shocked at her outburst. "I didn't know where else to put her when she didn't have a kingdom." That's another lie. "She's the only siren and when she came here, I knew she'd be of great companionship." Allah chooses his words carefully, knowing Amari can blow up on him and strip him of his titles. He shrugs. "There wasn't anything else for her, so I put her to work as a maid." That's another lie!

Allah knew *exactly* where to put Sirena considering she came here as a siren after her death. She's from Amari's dad's side of the family, the side that has no royalty to this world. Henceforth, Allah put her in with the maids.

"That's still beneath you," Amari barks. "Like you said! She's the first siren! She deserves to be treated as royalty, because that's what she is!"

Allah has no idea what to say or do next. He doesn't know Amari that well and has no idea if she needs to be seduced in some way or just be left to let it all out. Allah decides to try and go with the first tactic even though he can't think of Amari that way. He doesn't want to!

"Amari. Sweetie." Allah starts.

"Don't you dare 'sweetie' me. You don't get to seduce me!"

*Seriously,* Sirena starts as she slips into Allah's head without warning, creating a mind link. How did she do that? *Mark your mate and claim her at the throne. It'd be better that way.*

*Shut up, Sirena!* Allah snaps. He cuts the mind link off before Sirena can say anymore insanities. He leans over and takes Amari's hand in his, curling his fingers around her palm. "Tell me what I can do to turn this around."

Amari curls her fingers in and scratches the table. "What did I just say?" She threatens through clenched teeth.

Allah shakes his head at Amari, warning her not to cause a scene.

"Take your hand," Amari snaps threateningly. "Off me!" She's not playing whatsoever, ready to kill Allah.

Allah takes his hand back and does what's best at this point. Let Amari let it out and calm herself down.

"I, Amari Rose Greenwood," Amari starts addressing in an authoritative tone.

Shit. Allah shakes his head at Amari, not wanting to lose any of his titles. He's going to age fast once she demotes him as God of the were-kind!

"Queen and rightful heir of Hallam."

Fuck. Here it comes.

"Promote Sirena."

Oh, thank goddess!

"Daughter of the moon goddess herself. As queen of the sirens in the rivers, lakes, oceans, and seas. And next in line. To be goddess of the were-kind."

Fuck! Amari just bound Sirena here for good! She won't be dying suddenly in twenty-four years! She's here to stay! Sirena is heard behind Amari, moaning in pleasure. Allah looks back at her to see her head hanging from her shoulders.

"And I also hereby," Amari continues in her authoritative tone.

Allah tenses up and looks at Amari in fear.

"Create her equal. Her husband from Homba. As her siren mate and king. Consider both of them crowned."

Sirena gasps in delightful pleasure and Allah watches as water swirls around next to her, starting from the bottom and creating a waterspout that only consists of expanding water. It bursts and dissipates after a moment, making Sirena yell out in pleasure with her head thrown back.

A man four inches taller than her takes his first breath after being reborn from water, standing next to her. He looks at Sirena, dressed in bloody clothes and his dark brown hair in a disheveled mess.

"Sirena," the man says, happy to see his wife.

Sirena slowly lifts her head and looks at the man in front of her. "Matt!" She throws her arms around his neck and his arms instantly wrap around her waist. "Oh, my goddess!"

"What happened? One moment I was being tortured in hell and now I'm here!"

"You're bound to a new world, now. But here. Come sit with me and I will tell you everything."

"Shall I continue," Amari asks with a low devilish seductive tone.

Allah looks at Amari as Sirena and her reborned husband walk hand in hand to the maids' quarters. His silver-gray eyes meet with her brown eyes and he knows exactly where she's about to go.

"No." Allah reaches over and takes Amari's hand in his, his fingers curled around her palm, in hopes that she'll stop there and not demote Allah. "You're good. You got your wish. You're…"

Amari glances at Allah's hand curled over hers then she looks at him. He clears his throat and takes his hand back.

"Good." Allah finishes. He clears his throat and withdraws into himself, Ragnar howling inside to be close to Amari.

*Shut up, Ragnar. This is as close as you're gonna get!* He tries to knock some sense into his wolf. But Ragnar doesn't listen. He continues to howl as if he's howling to the moon. *Quiet, Ragnar!* Allah spats. *You're going to make my head explode!*

*I can't!* Ragnar sounds to be in pain. Is he okay? Ragnar continues to howl as the cooks come out with lunch on a food trolley.

*Ragnar! Quit howling!*

*You think I can control this?!*

*Of course, you can! You're Ragnar! King of all kings!*

Ragnar's legs shake as he continues to howl in pain, wanting Amari.

*Ragnar! Stop being so childish! She's right here!*

*She's not close enough! The sparks!*

Allah shakes his head at Ragnar. *I've learned to ignore them! You need to do the same!*

Ragnar yelps in pain as if Allah just pinched him in the withers. Ragnar barks at Allah. *Back off, old man! I hurt! I can't control it! Now, give me Amari!*

Allah stands up as his pulled barbeque pork sandwich with provolone cheese and grilled onion is put in front of him.

He sets his white towel on the table. "Excuse me." Allah clears his throat and he walks out of the dining room as Ragnar continues to pace, howl, whine, and shake in Allah's head.

"Get a hold of yourself, Ragnar," Allah snaps quietly until he can get to his office. "This is ridiculous!"

*No! You're ridiculous! You need to mark her!*

"I can't just mark her! She's the goddess of Hallam!"

*Not yet! So, I advise you to do what Sirena suggested you to do! Claim her!*

"No, Ragnar!" Allah gets up the stairs then quickly gets in his soundproof office with his key. He closes the door behind him. "I can't. And why are you feeling so much pain over this all of a sudden?"

"Maybe because of the mark on your neck," an all too familiar female voice says, sounding amused.

Allah stares at the woman sitting on his desk. The woman that decided to give him Amari as his second chance mate. Selena. His first wife and love. And his one and only moon goddess that died several years ago.

## 13

Amari takes a bite of her delicious barbeque pulled pork sandwich and all the flavors mingle together. Barbeque, brown sugar, toasted wheat, butter, pork, grilled onion, and melted provolone cheese all melt in Amari's mouth and she moans with pleasure, closing her eyes and slowly hanging her head back.

Sometimes she thinks she's Joey from F·R·I·E·N·D·S. She loves food and she loves women. But the only difference is that she doesn't sleep around. She's serious about what she said to Amy. Amy has no idea the kind of trouble she just put herself in. She's going back to Amari's estate once this war with Kera is over. And Allah will never see her, again.

But why does she want Lexi to come with? Does Lexi get bullied here? She has a husband, but yet it seems Marcus is afraid to mark her. Amari growls at the thought of one of her creatures being mistreated, knowing damn well why Marcus is afraid to mark his own mate. But how many are actually getting bullied? Does Amari need to put in an investigation? She has the best resources if she needs to do that.

Amari puts her sandwich down as she starts to lose her appetite and she brings her head down. She stares at the wall and swallows her chewed up bite. Maybe she should wait for Allah. Should she maybe wait for Sirena and Matt as well? Will they be joining? Amari puts her sandwich down on her plate and she wipes her hands with her napkin. She should go find Allah.

∞

Amy's hands run down her mate's body and grope her ass, bringing the other woman's hips flush against Amy's hips and making Amy slip way too easily inside of her.

She knows this is wrong… But they're fated mates for a reason. Being fated mates has to mean something! Amy knows how it hurt her when Amy had sex with Amari just moments ago.

Never. Again. Amy hopes Amari can forgive her. Amy thrusts into her mate at a slow pace, wanting to make it up to her and love her all day and night. Amy wants to fill her with her seed and get her pregnant this time. It's what they've been wanting for twelve years, now. A family.

With no hate or judgment from others. Amy's mate squirms underneath her, wanting to cry out her release. She throws her head back.

"Uh," her mate squeals.

"Shh," Amy shushes her mate. She puts her lips on the spot where there should be a mate mark. But Amy and her mate have been too nervous to mark each other, afraid of everyone figuring it out.

Senses heightened because of the mate bond, Amy groans in her mate's ear. She's trying so hard not to scream out her mate's name. So, she does the only thing she can think of doing. Their naked breasts pressed together their legs stay entangled as Amy moves her lips to her mate's shoulder. She bites down hard. Her mate starts to scream in pure bliss and Amy's hand swiftly moves straight to her mouth to quiet her.

Her mate pants heavily into her hand, trying to regain her composure. Luckily, they're in Amari's estate, where it looks like nobody is here. But they could never be too cautious of their surroundings. Amy's mate moans into her hand loudly as she thrusts into her harder.

"Amy," her mate calls out into her hand. "Fuck me, Amy! Harder!"

Amy growls as her primal instincts kick in and she kisses her mate, the kiss passionate, hot, and steamy. Amy wraps her arms around her mate's arms and lays her hands on her shoulders. She pauses for a moment, the tip of her cock barely inside of her mate.

*What are you doing,* Amy's mate asks in a mind link.

*Listening,* Amy replies. *With that scream someone could've heard.*

Amy's mate nods her head and they both quiet. They heighten their hearing to double check they're completely alone. After a couple of minutes of dead silence, they get the confirmation. They're completely alone.

Amy smiles at her mate and her mate gives her the same smile. Amy thrusts into her mate, bringing her down by the shoulders and ramming into her so hard pure bliss comes over the both of them and for once they're able to scream and yell their words of pleasure for each other.

Amy has the time of her life as she makes love to her mate and they kiss as Amy continues to rail into her mate like her life depends on it, the headboard of some maid's bed banging into the wall very loudly. They can't stop the multiple orgasms that come and Amy's eyes flutter, unable to control herself as she lets herself go just this once.

She winds up spilling a massive amount of her seed into her mate, screaming out her mate's name to the walls. Fuck, she loves her! And there's no one else for her!

Amy's mate moans as she starts to come to.

"I'm gonna have your baby," she whispers. Amy smiles at the thought, her lips on her mate's lips as she shows her pearly white time. Their twin blue eyes bare into each other. Amy nods her head.

"With Amari we'll be safe," Amy whispers. "And you'll be able to have *all* my kids."

"Oh, Mommy," she moans, wrapping her arms around Amy's neck. "I can't wait."

Amy and her mate kiss. She thrusts into her mate one last time before she goes limp from her release.

∞

"Selena," Allah says, dumbstruck.

How is she…? She died! She's not supposed to be able to come down! Oh, but she looks more beautiful than ever. Her choice of clothes are… Revealing. Wearing a v-neck crop top that shows too much and short shorts that practically show off her ass.

"Hi, hubby," Selena says, batting her eyelashes like she used to do. "Miss me, love?"

"More than anything," Allah finally manages out. "How did you…?" He trails off.

"Oh, this isn't my body. It's my doppelganger's."

"Uh." Allah drags out. He points at Selena, trying to figure out everything that's staring him right in the face.

"Don't worry." Selena continues to hold her position on Allah's desk, one leg propped up on it with her foot on the desk and the other hanging in front of his desk. "I don't plan on letting her know where you live or put Amari in danger of a mermaid in crisis."

"So, what are you doing here? To taunt me in that outfit? You know, it doesn't suit you."

Selena grunts in disgust and throws her head back. "I know. It's quite disgusting if you ask me. But it's what she wears and I can't change it just for me. Besides." Selena looks at Allah, her hands on the desk. "I came to help you with your crisis at hand."

Allah finally drops his hand, keeping his eyes on his beloved wife. Well… Her doppelganger that has her spirit in it. "You said something about my mate mark being the issue with Ragnar's suffering."

"Yes."

"Can you please clarify why?"

"Amari accidentally marked you with her breath. She didn't mean to. She wants *nothing* romantic with you." Selena sounds like she's having fun with this.

"Well, there's something she and I have in common." Allah shakes his head as he tries to get to the bottom of things. He furrows his eyebrows.

"But." Selena brings her leg down and she hangs both legs over Allah's desk, her violet eyes dead set on him with her legs dangling over the front of the desk.

"No." Allah shakes his head. "No, but's Selena."

"She doesn't have one-night stands."

Allah winces. "Fuck."

Selena nods her head. "Yeah. You're in trouble. She's trying to make it work with you because of it, but you keep messing it up. And you're about to be demoted to nothing if you're not careful."

Allah nods his head. "Okay. Just tell me what to do about the mate mark."

"Get rid of it. Or make it work."

Allah winces. He doesn't like any of those options! He couldn't lose the connection he now has with Amari! It helps him know how she feels to better accommodate the situation! But Allah couldn't mark his goddess either!

"Or Ragnar will be in pain every time you're near her because she doesn't bare your mark."

"Is-is there another op-option?" Allah stutters. He doesn't like where this is going.

"Mark each other and forever feel pain when the other has sex with their mistress or significant other. Your call."

Allah shakes his head in confusion, his eyebrows furrowed. What is this? Some kind of show? "I don't see how that's an option."

Selena shrugs. "Call it as it is." Selena perks her head up as the doorknob shakes.

Allah looks back at the shaking doorknob. *Amari, is that you?* He mind links with Amari with ease.

*Yeah!* Amari's answer comes fast. *I decided to wait for you to come back down. But we do need to talk. In private.*

*Alright, I'll let you in.* Allah looks back at Selena, but she's gone.

Heartbreak settles in. Allah wanted to kiss her one last time, give her a proper farewell since he wasn't able to the day she died. He wasn't there when it happened. Allah walks over to the door and he unlocks it. One second later he's opening the door towards him. Amari tumbles into him. He catches her in his arms.

"Geez! What were you doing? Hanging on the door?"

"I guess I'm caught red handed," Amari drawls out, her eyes meeting Allah's. "I was trying to eavesdrop."

"Soundproof walls."

"I figured." Amari pulls out of Allah's arms and walks into his office. "So." She turns around in the middle of Allah's office and looks at him. With Selena's dress on she looks like she's mourning for someone. And who knows? She probably is mourning for someone back in Homba. But she looks so damn good in that dress.

The dress is only in two parts. There's the tube top silk dress and then the lace. With its slim body it hugs all of the right curves on Amari. Her left leg slips through the slit in the dress as she bends her leg and leans back into her other leg, her thigh being exposed and reminding Allah of what they did just twenty-four hours ago.

He shudders as he tries not to remember. But Amari's skin is pressing into him, again, and he has the drive to get one of Ada's eggs inside of her fertilized. Allah tries not to remember how good Amari felt and how her body fit just right into place against his.

"Are any of the creatures here getting bullied," Amari asks in a low, husky tone. She throws Allah off with her question and he winces.

"Uh," he drawls out. His lips part to show the shock he feels at the question.

"It's a quick yes or no question, Allah."

Allah shakes his head, trying to gain back his composure. Damn it, Amari! With your caring and watchful heart for his world you sure know how to get a stubborn man going with just one question!

"No." Allah defends himself. "No. Nothing like that conspires here."

"Then why is Lexi so mistreated Amy feels like she has to protect her?"

"She's not mistreated." Allah closes the door behind him and locks it. "Some of my men just think they can use her for a release since she's not mated to anyone."

"And what if she is?"

Allah winces. "Then she would have her mate mark."

"Here's the thing, Allah." Amari doesn't sound amused and she most definitely doesn't show any signs of *looking* to be amused. "Anymore the creatures of Hallam are afraid to claim their omega mate. In fear of being demoted. What if he's your beta or delta and he doesn't want to disappoint you?"

"Then he should step forward and claim his prize." Allah starts for Amari and she backs up to keep the distance between them. "Because no lycan of mine should be mate-less. And he'll have his way with his mate."

"I feel like this conversation is going off course."

"Oh, no, Amari. This conversation has stayed on course. It's you're questioning my motives for my world that's getting you dangerously close to the cliff that I'll *personally* throw you off."

Amari's backside meets the front of Allah's desk and, for once, his conversation with her is going his way. The only problem is Ragnar growling and writhing in pain.

"I suggest you tread lightly." Allah stands right in front of Amari and he instantly leans in to trap her between him and his desk, his arms on either side of her. "And ask me a different question."

"Like why you wanna expand," Amari mumbles. Her eyes flicker from Allah's lips to his eyes and he knows what she's thinking of doing to get out of this situation.

Allah chuckles, his chuckle deep in his chest. He watches how it unravels Amari at the core, her eyes betraying her of her motives. Allah leans in and lets his lips tickle Amari's, his silver-gray eyes piercing her brown eyes. Her body relaxes into his for once.

"For the good of the world. More grounds and waters mean more life for your creatures. And less battles over territory."

Amari sighs with her lips parted, her breath tickling Allah's lips. "Why do you have to be so damn hot?"

"You tell me," Allah says roughly. "You're the one that likes older men."

Amari's eyes look down, but she doesn't move her lips and they feather against Allah's, sending sparks and fireworks through his body and making Ragnar relax at ease.

"I do," Amari barely manages out in softness. "I like my men older and my women my age. There's a reason for it."

"I bet I can change that," Allah finds himself seducing Amari. It feels good to have her so close. Her scent soothes his nerves and puts his wolf at ease. One kiss and Allah will be deep inside of Amari and Ragnar will be healed. But he wouldn't be able to stop himself from spilling his seed inside of her.

"How so," Amari presses, as if she's already tried to ask her question once before.

"I can change your preference to just men. And you'll be so straight you'll forget you were ever bi."

"Oh?" Amari whispers softly. "And why do you say that?"

"Because I'll be there to remind you every. Single. Night."

Amari nods her head and her lips send healing energy through Allah's body.

*Closer, Allah,* Ragnar howls in Allah's head. *I need to feel her!*

"We're back to twenty-fours ago, are we?" Amari seduces lowly.

"Don't tempt me," Allah mumbles, almost growling. He feels his member get excited.

Amari gets seductive and sits on Allah's desk, her hand sneaking around his face and their lips clashing together. Allah breathes in Amari's scent through his nose and he lets it take over him. Ragnar celebrates at Amari's touch, but he still howls for a release.

Oh, Allah will give it to him! What Ragnar wants Ragnar gets! Allah won't mark Amari, but he knows a physical release will do for Ragnar. Allah unbuckles his belt. Amari's free hand trails up his chest. She better be ready for him! Cause he's not going to go easy on her this time!

Allah unzips his pants and unbuttons the button on them with one swift move.

*Wait!* Ragnar yells. *Don't rush it! She's not ready!*

*She's going to have to be!* Allah orders Ragnar. *It's this or nothing when we're in close range with her like this!*

*I don't want it like this!* Ragnar snarls at Allah.

Amari's fingers tangle in Allah's hair and she sparks something inside of him. Something that drives Ragnar crazy. Oh, her touch does things to him.

*It's the only way, Ragnar,* Allah finally replies to Ragnar, who is pacing with energy and a new motive.

What that motive is Allah has no clue. Ragnar won't let him in. Allah shoves his pants and boxers down and his member springs free from its barriers, ready for Amari's tight wetness.

Allah's hand sneaks into the dress and he strokes Amari's vulva, finding out that she's more than ready for him.

"Allah," Amari whispers in his ear as his lips make their way down her neck.

He doesn't know what he's doing. He just knows he's letting Ragnar feel Amari. Allah doesn't pay attention to where his lips roam on Amari. He's just happy to put his wolf at ease. Allah slips two of his big fingers inside of

Amari and she gasps. Her breath turns ragged, her panting heavy as Allah fucks her opening with his fingers.

He gets so caught up with her opening herself up to him he doesn't realize what he's doing with his mouth on her spot until it's too late. Ragnar has let his fangs grow in Allah's mouth, who takes a deep breath before sinking them into Amari's neck, caught in the moment. Amari gasps as the new sensation comes over her.

She reacts too late, Allah thrusting her hips into his, so he's flush with her body, his massive pulsing cock inside of her. She yells in what seems to be short-lived pleasure as he fills her completely.

"Allah!" Amari shoves on Allah's chest, pushing him back and putting her hand to her neck. "What the fuck did you just do?" She growls with a glare.

Allah stares at Amari as she holds her neck. What did he just do? He asks himself. Then it hits him. *Ragnar, what did you just do?* He growls at his wolf.

*What any sane wolf and king would do,* Ragnar replies. *Do the rational thing.*

*No, Ragnar!*

*She's officially ours! It's what we both wanted!*

*No!* Allah growls in anger. He didn't want this! In between Amari's legs, he forgets he's deep inside of her.

Amari quickly looks around Allah's desk for something shiny, her hand over her mate mark spot on her neck. Allah doesn't need to look to know what's underneath. He already knows by instinct.

Amari pulls Allah's flask out of the top drawer on the left side of his desk. She pulls her hand away from her neck and gold wings behind a gold wolf's head stare Allah in the face.

*Ragnar, what have you done?* Allah stares in horror. *We're done for!*

*I needed a better release!* Ragnar defends himself. *I couldn't let you rape Amari for me!*

*Rape?! How do you call this rape? She gladly obliged!*

*I was in her head!* Ragnar snaps, pacing in Allah's head as Amari stares at the reflection of her mark in his flask. *She couldn't do it! Not when she's so in love with Garrett!*

*That's not how she felt yesterday!* Allah defends himself. He starts shaking his head.

*She was doing it against her own will to save us, Allah! She* forced *herself on us! For us! You know this! You know* her! Ragnar snarls as he looks at Allah and his gold eyes glow. *You! Just forced yourself. On her! This time! And she's not going to forgive you for this! I can assure you of that!*

"Amari," Allah mutters. "I'm so…"

Amari puts her hand to her mouth, tears in her eyes. She stares at the reflection of Allah's mark. What has he done? Allah acts on instinct and he wraps his arms around Amari. But she shoves him off of her, making his cock pull out of her. She gets down from his desk.

"Amari, it was Ragnar," Allah defends himself. "He was in con-."

"Don't," Amari snaps, cutting Allah off and pointing at him with a look of disgust on her face. Her body twisted towards him he watches her break inside, her eyes showing how furious she is. "Blame it on Ragnar. You wanted this! You wanted me marked! And then some! You want me to bear your children for Ada?! Forget it! I'm getting rid. Of every single one of her eggs! You're done with her! And you're done with me! You'll be lucky if I don't strip you of *both* of your titles tonight!"

"Amari, I can explain." Allah turns towards Amari as she starts to leave.

She looks at his massive cock that's sprung from its barriers and ready for a release. "You call that!" She points at it while her furious eyes meet with his calm eyes. "Explainable?! Allah?!" Amari shakes her head. "Get it in your head, Allah! I don't want you! I have a mistress and boyfriend out in a war without my back up right now! My priority is them!"

Amari points at the wall with a couple of in-wall bookcases, but Allah imagines she's actually pointing towards where she thinks her estate is. "My priority is my people! And their safety! I'm in love with Garrett! And I love Ada! Not you!" Amari points down at the floor in front of her, her glare on Allah so full of hatred he's convinced he'll be stripped of all that he has in just one hour.

Allah starts to regret ever going to Amari's estate yesterday to confront the woman Ada was doing it with. He should've just dealt with the pain and let Ada be happy!

"It will never be you, Allah! I'm done with you!" "Amari. Stop. You're just acting out on rage, right now. Don't say something you're going to regret."

"Then put it away, Allah!" Amari orders in a voice so strong Allah listens right away.

Ragnar whimpers inside of Allah's head, truly afraid of what Amari is going to do. *This is your doing, Ragnar!* Allah snaps at his wolf as he arranges his pulsing cock into his pants.

"You might smell good! You might be irresistible at times! And yes! I care about you! But I'm! In love! With my! Officiant! Were you ever there for me in a time of need?!"

"No."

"No!" Amari screams. "That's right, Allah! No! So, back the fuck off!"

"It was Ragnar, Amari." Allah tries to defend himself. "He was in pain. Every time I'm near you he wreathes in pain, because you marked us and wouldn't let us mark you."

"I did that! On *fuckin'* accident, Allah! I had no idea I had that effect with just my breath!" Amari shakes her head as she shakes in anger with tears streaming down her face. Her actions and words say it all. She was only drawn to Allah because of the mate pull. Nothing else. "I'm leaving. Tonight. As of this moment you're of no concern to me." Amari shakes her head, again.

"You're not my mate," she growls. Amari walks over to the door and unlocks it. Then she strides out of Allah's office, leaving him behind.

His heart breaks, his heart proving to Allah he felt something for this woman and he was just too stubborn to see it. Amari was there to try and save his son when he received gashes on his arms and chest that ran so deep, he bled out and died in her arms.

Amari was the one in bloody clothes as she delivered Allah's nine-year-old, freshly turned son in her arms. His arms falling limp out of the blanket she had him wrapped in while all of his blood was all over her clothes. A lycan at the age of nine can easily be mistaken as an adult werewolf since it's the lycan creature that's born first. Before the wolf is born.

Madi made that mistake with Allah's son and it took Amari a lot of convincing to change Allah's mind about his son's killer. Amari crowned all the lycan kings and she crowned Allah as God of all were-kind. Amari walked in Allah's gardens with him whenever he couldn't sleep and they talked business. She knew to never bring up his son's death, since Zack was his only child.

They rarely talked about Amari's life, but when they did Mike was always up to something. The next time Amari and Allah would talk business he would always ask her if she ever found out what Mike was up to. It would always wind up being a surprise date where it was just the two of them alone without any distractions, having dinner in just the candlelight and catching up on their favorite shows together. Mike was a gentleman before he left on his mission. When he came back home, he was changed. And he got overly protective of Amari.

Allah remembers to breathe and he takes a breath. He sighs, tears in his eyes. His thoughts go back to yesterday. Allah had a vengeance. To kill Amari and be done with her stupidity. He didn't like how she got so stupid with Mike. And then with Ada…

Allah couldn't control himself. Or Ragnar. Amari would be dead if it wasn't for Sunni. And then the way she came to Allah's rescue in the forest. He's an idiot. He's a fuckin' idiot! Why would Amari sacrifice so much for him just to save him? They were never lovers! And they were nowhere close to being friends before! They were just business partners!

Amari is a saint. And Allah drove her over the edge with his stupidity. By letting Ragnar take over.

*I thought I was doing the right thing!* Ragnar howls inside Allah's head. He sounds broken. *I didn't mean for it to go this far!*

"Yeah?" Allah challenges Ragnar. "Well, whose damn fault is that?"

*You need to go stop her!*

"Why?" Allah growls. "She want's nothing to do with us."

*Kera, you idiot!* Kera… Allah looks up in realization as he remembers what Amari said before she walked out. She's not leaving tonight!

"Amari," Allah calls out, drawing out his second chance mate's name as he goes after her. "Wait!"

# 14

Garrett hears his men and women outside of his tent. They're all hanging out together like a homeless family in a village they've made for themselves. They decided to stick together and just send one homeless looking person to check on the estate to make sure everything still looks good.

Tents are spread out while axes are being thrown at wood during the day and food is being caught every day to make it look like homeless people are making themselves a new village on land to claim as their own. Garrett and his team were made for this. Built for this. They know how to survive in the wild thanks to their backgrounds and lineage.

Garrett throws the door to his tent open and he watches Baron start a small fire in the middle of camp with kindling he found in the woods and two small logs. They don't want to draw attention to themselves with a big fire so they keep it small and just make coals for their meals. They share their rabbits, squirrels, and doves with each other, knowing they can't hunt for anything bigger. Or Kera would know they're Amari's security. Garrett knows this by experience.

He steps out of his tent and closes the door behind him. He grabs his stump and carving he's been working on for Amari and gets working on it with his pocket knife, sitting on his stump. Baron joins him, sitting next to him on his stump with the small fire burning to make coals.

"Are you gonna eat real food tonight," Baron asks, looking at Garrett. "Maya's caught a few rabbits earlier."

"Nah," Garrett replies, drawing the word out. He's been so worried about Amari and her safety. He knows she can hold her own and defend herself, but he's so love stricken and worried about her he missed a rabbit with his sling shot earlier. He was too slow to strike.

"So, it's Cheez-its and sardines again tonight, huh?"

"Actually, no." Garrett replies.

"Then what are you eating?"

"Jerky." Garrett grabs his bag of deer jerky. "Want some? It's homemade."

Baron takes a moment to consider before taking a piece of jerky from Garrett's Ziploc bag. "Did Erika make this?"

"No." Garrett sets his Ziploc bag down and gets back to whittling. "I did. I went hunting during deer season. Got me an eight point."

"Nice!"

"Had a pair of extra antlers too so it was a win-win."

"What were they?"

"Six point. Not as impressive."

"Well, sounds like it was a fair fight considering the outcome."

"Well… Second buck was already dead. Snapped its neck."

"Did you call it in?" Baron sounds impressed.

"Oh, yeah."

"And?" Baron presses, showing he's too interested in this conversation.

Garrett looks up at the village in front of him. "I got a free buck out of it. Luckily, they were fighting moments before I took the shot. So, he was fresh."

Baron laughs, not surprised. "Garrett, you have the best luck. No wonder you landed as Amari's official suitor."

Garrett shrugs, making an uncertain sound. "I get to spend the most time with her besides Adam. But he's married."

"Only because you two get to cross over. Where's he at, anyway? I haven't seen him here, yet."

"Other side of the world chasing Kera. She was spotted with Mike over there so he took some men with him."

"Is Amari going to join pursuit?"

"No." Garrett looks at his little carving that's taken shape. He's been working on it for Amari ever since she came here. "She strongly believes Kera will come challenge her."

"I'm not surprised. Amari wants her dead the most. Raja had to pull her off the witch."

"I just hope Alia and Amelia haven't gotten involved with her."

"They're her daughters. I'm sure she's looking for them."

"Yep." Garrett nods his head, his eyes on his carving.

A branch is heard being snapped in the forest and everyone hears it. They all stop and go quiet, waiting for a sign of life to come out. Garrett looks behind Maya's tent and he sees movement. A moment later, Adam and only a few of his men rush into the village while looking back and staying quiet. Adam sends a silent message to everyone in camp to get down or hidden, his gun across his chest and his arm motioning towards the ground with his palm down.

Garrett instantly gets in his tent and grabs his gun. He hides behind the flap and barely peeks the small round barrel of his gun out. His people do the same. Adam joins him in his tent after his gun is set up and Adam points his gun ahead of him. Not a word is said. They don't even sign to each other to converse.

Everything is quiet, making Garrett wonder if it's a false alarm. But then it comes out of the forest. A creature that looks like a deathwalker, its legs looking like brittle bone. Garrett holds his breath. Spiritwalker. The original shapeshifter. These creatures are rare. And created by Amari when she had a nightmare about them as a kid. Spiritwalkers are not meant to be messed with. They roamed on Hallam for a while. But during the war with Kera, they went into hiding. And no one has seen one until now.

What's it doing so close to civilization? These creatures are lone creatures that never socialize! They prefer to stay in their caves and only come out to fight off intruders. But there's no caves in this area. This spiritwalker is far from home. What Garrett wants to know is why.

Garrett looks through the small scope of his gun and puts his finger on the trigger. If it so much looks this way, he's going to shoot it. The senses on a spiritwalker are like no other shapeshifters. It can smell you from miles away and the small hairs on its body can sense vibrations almost a mile away. So why this spiritwalker hasn't attacked Adam and his few men that are left is a mystery. The spiritwalker, in a form of a deathwalker, stops and turns around to face the village.

It cocks its flat face as it stares right at Garrett and he wonders what it's thinking. Is it going to attack? Adam stiffens next to Garrett and it's as if all life stops making noise, being sucked into silence.

Garrett waits for the spiritwalker to make a move. It's as if it gets in his head, making him stiffen. But he feels the presence of a very familiar human being as if he knows it.

*I'm on your side,* a strange but yet familiar voice says in Garrett's mind.

Garrett lifts his head and he lets his gray eyes stare right into the eyes of the spiritwalker.

*A war is coming. Amari and Madison must be crowned before it comes. Please… You don't have much time left.*

Garrett looks at Adam and their eyes meet. Every gun in camp is heard being put down, but nobody comes out of hiding. A rustling in the forest is heard and snaps Garrett's and Adam's attention. They look toward the sound, the spiritwalker gone.

Garrett lifts his chin in confidence, knowing this war that's coming is bigger than the last.

And everybody needs to be ready for it.

∞

Adam hangs his head after a moment, letting it lay on his arm. That was a close one! Oh… Hallelujah! Adam wonders why that spiritwalker didn't come after him and his men. Spiritwalkers are usually very aggressive! Mean to the core! Did they change somehow? Adam doesn't think about it for long as a hand grips his shoulder and his heart stops, thinking the spiritwalker decided to come back.

"Adam," Garrett whispers, confirming that the spiritwalker is gone. Nobody dares talk or move when one is close by in fear of getting eaten. "Where are all of your men?"

"In the belly of a titan snake," Adam mumbles. "The few of us are lucky to have gotten away."

"Kera."

Adam nods his head, his eyes closed. "Mhmm."

"That bitch." Garrett growls.

"We've been on her tail this whole entire time. And we've been trying to figure out why she would come back here."

"Amari."

Adam opens his eyes and looks up at Garrett, his tired mind wanting some rest. He didn't think of that. "We need to…"

"Don't worry. She's at Allah's for now."

Adam nods his head, grateful for his best friend's safety. "I think we need to get her crowned. Right away."

"Madison first. I fear as though if I don't crown Madi it will never happen."

"That's right. You can crown the god and goddess for anything. But Viggo is…"

"Can only crown Amari. I've been training him to be the next officiator for all life here. I mean… He's immortal and can't get killed so easily. Me, on the other hand…"

"You're only human."

Garrett nods his head. "With power."

"Are you going to be okay with me as the next commander? I know we have our differences and all…"

Garrett nods his head. "You're perfect, Adam. You've been a great apprentice. Even though I hate your pranks."

Adam laughs and rolls onto his back. He moans… "Can I just… Take a little nap? I've been up for more than seventy-two hours. Following Kera."

"Yeah." Garrett puts his gun down next to his air mattress then slaps Adam's gut, making him grunt. "Get some sleep. We'll be having dinner in a while."

"Thank you, Dad."

Garrett gets out of his tent. "You're welcome." Garrett leaves Adam in his tent and Adam lets himself drift into sleep, where he's greeted with his wife's face and their little three-year-old Mazie.

∞

"Amari," Allah calls in the distance. He doesn't sound too far away, close enough for Amari to cringe. Can't he just leave her alone!

In the forest that's on the left side of his castle, Amari decided to get away from Allah for the rest of the day before she heads out to fight alongside Viggo on the open sea. Amari is going to leave tonight instead of tomorrow night. Get an early start. She doesn't want to be near Allah right now. As much as she enjoys the mate pull, she's distressed that it has to be with Allah. Even though she feels something for him. But if anything, Amari wants to feel it with Garrett, who she loves more. But she never will feel the mate bond with him, considering that they're both just humans.

Amari's mind drifts to Garrett and memories of his smile and goofy demeanor help her relax. She could really use a hug from him right now! Garrett… Amari starts to reach out to him via mind link, but then chuffing sounds from behind her as a cat announces its presence, making some noise with a bush.

Amari looks back and her face gets covered right away with an orange and white head with stripes. Her arms instantly wrap around the tiger's neck. The familiarity is way too much. The markings. The chuff. The moan… It's her… And about damn time! Where has she been?!

"Raja, girl," Amari says in relief, burying her face in her companion's neck. "Oh, I've missed you."

Raja moans, letting Amari know she's missed her companion as well. Amari moans, her eyes closed against Raja's fur.

"It's about damn time," she whispers.

Raja chuffs and starts to shrink down to her size for Homba. Amari pulls back and watches her. Raja starts to rub up against Amari with her body. She rubs her head on Amari's hip. Raja turns her head so her forehead is pressed against Amari.

Amari laughs, knowing what Raja is doing. Marking her territory and letting anyone who dares to touch Amari know that they will be met with their fate.

"Oh, Raja," Amari moans. "I love you."

Raja moans and walks around Amari, who watches her as she circles her companion. She's quiet for the most part. Something seems to be up.

"You wanna go for a ride," Amari breathes, watching her feline best friend.

Raja nods her head briefly and takes a few steps in front of Amari. She looks back at her favorite human, waiting for her. Amari nods.

"Let's go." Amari walks over to Raja's side and swings her leg over her. Amari gets settled on Raja's back then Raja grows into her Hallam size, standing just a few inches taller than Amari on foot. Her shoulder meets the height of Amari's head if Amari were to stand next to her.

Raja pushes forward as Amari leans down to grab onto her long fur around her neck and keeps her legs on either side of Raja. Amari feels the wind in her face and she can't help but notice how she is one with her spirit animal. Amari can feel Raja's legs moving as if they're her own, pushing with power and burning with a sensation that makes her wanna run even faster.

Raja pushes off the ground and into the air. Her claws sink into a tree trunk for a moment before she pushes off of it and veers left for a different direction. What was that about? Amari looks back as she hears a snarl and her eyes meet Ragnar's, who has a death glare on his face. Apparently, Ragnar is jealous! But that means... Fuck! Ragnar meets up with Raja and snaps his teeth at her. She growls a roar at him in warning, but he doesn't back down. Instead, it fuels him to go after her.

Amari summons one of her light swords and slashes it across Ragnar's shoulder before he can sink his canines into Raja's neck. He yelps and backs off, looking at Amari with apologetic but broken eyes. He looks to be in pain. Not from his wound that's already healing. But a broken heart split into two pieces. Amari slants her sword across her chest, warning Allah and Ragnar to back off. Ragnar listens and veers a different direction, putting space between him and Amari. She puts her sword away, sending it back to where it belongs. Heaven's Light's armory.

Once Amari is crowned as Hallam's Goddess that's where she will go. Her kingdom is up in Heaven's Light. But her estate will always be here in Hallam whenever she wants to come down and visit. Madi will be able to visit Hallam anytime she wants as well. But she and Amari will be so busy keeping their kingdoms running and at peace that they won't be able to visit Hallam as much as they want. And they'll be doing constant business with each other.

Raja continues to run and Amari holds onto her fur as they feel the wind on their faces, forgetting about Allah.

∞

Allah shifts and comes to a halt, still in the forest next to his castle. He stares ahead in disbelief. She hates him! She wants nothing to do with him! How could he be *so stupid?!* Allah should never have touched her back in his office! He should've kept his hands to himself! Kept his distance! What was he thinking?!

*Stop thinking about it!* Ragnar snarls, showing his canines. He glares at Allah. *What's done is done!*

"You're the one that marked her," Allah yells at Ragnar. "I just wanted to fuck her to help with your pain!"

*Yeah?!*

"Yeah! So, get over yourself! And I warned you not to go after Raja! But did you listen? No!"

Ragnar shifts through Allah's mind, appearing in the forest. Allah watches him pace around in front of him. The gash on Ragnar's shoulder made by Amari's sword gushes blood. Allah glares at him.

"Heal yourself."

Ragnar glares at Allah. "Why should I?" His voice echoes in the forest in a few different octaves. He's pissed. Why does Ragnar have to be so stubborn and bullheaded? He's the reason they're in this mess to begin with! He needs to calm down and think!

Allah sighs and sags as he remembers why Ragnar is so stubborn and bullheaded, looking at Ragnar in disbelief. Oh, that's right! They're the exact same! Curse this bond that *they* have. "You're an idiot. And because of that it's gonna get yourself killed."

"No." Ragnar picks up his paws as he paces around the clearing in the forest slowly. "Idiocy runs in your blood. Not mine!"

Allah keeps his eyes on his wolf, not wanting to lose sight of him. If Ragnar runs off, Allah will be with no wolf for who knows how long! This kind of out of body experience can only happen with lycans, thankfully. They have two forms to shapeshift into so their wolf can have some true time alone before they're ready to come back.

Allah can't stand the thought of losing Ragnar over this, though. Over Amari! While he loves her, he wants the best for her. And he's not sure if he can be with her right now. Ragnar keeps acting up with her nearby.

"Ragnar, listen to yourself," Allah says. "This isn't like you!"

"Leave it alone, Allah!" Ragnar snaps. His massive paws don't make a sound on the first leaves that have fallen onto the earth as he continues to pace, pissed off and anxious. "It's not your problem!"

"It is when I'm your human! Now, what's gotten into you all of a sudden?"

"That creature… Inside of Amari… It wants out, but it won't let me help it."

"Just give it some time, Ragnar. It'll surface with the right push."

"That's the part you don't understand!" Ragnar takes a leap towards Allah, turning. He crouches down as he shows his teeth in a snarl, just a few feet away from him. "We don't have that kind of time! And if Amari leaves tonight, we'll *never* get that time!"

"Well, who's fault is that?"

Ragnar growls at Allah, baring his teeth in a crouch.

"Fine!" Allah snaps, taking a step towards Ragnar as he keeps his gray eyes on Ragnar's golden eyes. "If you wanna go for a run, go for it! I'll convince Amari to stay one more night the old fashion way! I prefer it, anyway!"

"Go ahead without me! And I'll use that run! I need some time away from you anyway! You're so *stupid*!"

"No, Ragnar! We wouldn't be in this mess if it weren't for you! Or Selena! I would've happily died from the pain Ada caused me! I didn't want Amari! You did!"

Ragnar growls at Allah, ready to strike.

"Go for your run!" Allah spats. He turns his back to Ragnar. "And don't come back until you've come to your senses!" Allah starts for his castle and Ragnar snarls at him with a growl from behind.

Claws slice across Allah's naked back. He quickly turns around and thrusts his fist in an uppercut at Ragnar's open mouth, punching Ragnar's jaws and making his teeth sink into his tongue, making a hole there. Ragnar yelps and whines in pain. He slumps to the ground in defeat.

Allah shakes his head at Ragnar, his heart breaking at the sight of his beloved wolf in so much pain, tasting blood in his mouth. If he could, he would fix it. But he knows he can't. Ragnar is so hung up on Amari, he can't think straight! Some space and time away from her would do him some good.

Ragnar crumbles underneath Allah's broken and forgiving stare. Allah bends down and ignores the stinging pain in his back.

"Oh, Ragnar," Allah sighs, pulling his wolf's head into his arms. He buries his face in Ragnar's silver-gray fur. "You're an idiot, but I love you." Allah lets his hand run down Ragnar's body, his fingers entangling in Ragnar's fur. "You're *my* idiot."

Ragnar lifts his head in a sad attempt to look at Allah, who lays his head on his best friend's head. Allah forces Ragnar's head to lay back down and he hugs Ragnar's neck, his face in Ragnar's fur. Allah grabs onto Ragnar's soft fur with a reassuring squeeze.

"Take care of yourself, old friend," Allah whispers. "I'll be back for you when you're ready. Just give me a howl when you are." Allah lets go of Ragnar and starts for his castle.

He hates leaving his best friend behind when he's so broken, his heart breaking for him. But Allah's got to do what's best for Ragnar. Cast him out of his mind so he can save the little bit that's left to gain Amari's favor.

# 15

Amari knocks on the door of Allah's bedroom, not wanting to be here. But he asked her to come talk to him via a mind link. Nicely and sounding like himself. Something must have happened for him to finally come to his senses.

Was it maybe when Amari warned him off back in the forest? Or did something happen afterwards? Either way, she's glad to hear that he's back to his old self.

*Come in,* Allah says in a successful mind link. Amari opens the door to find Allah's naked back to her. Luckily, he has pants on. But his back has four gashes that are bright red, two of the gashes close together.

Seeing that he's okay and already healing, Amari doesn't worry too much. But she still wonders what happened and if she can help Allah with anything. There she goes, again! Why does she have to have such a big heart?!

"What happened," Amari mumbles.

"Nothing," Allah mumbles from across the room as he does something at his small side table.

"It's not nothing, Allah. You've four bright red marks on your back."

Allah continues to sign some papers and set them aside, ignoring Amari for a moment. "Yes. Well." He finally speaks up in a low tone. "Not everything is your business, now, is it?"

Amari winces at Allah's coldness as she closes the door behind her, wondering if what she did to ward him off made him act this cold towards her. But she can still treat him the same way with what happened not too long ago.

Amari looks at Allah's back and that's when she finally pays attention to the spacing of the gashes. A wolf got him. Ragnar. It had to be considering he was the only wolf who would go after Allah! No other werewolf or lycan will go up against him!

"You got in a fight with your wolf," Amari spoke up.

"Why do you think that is?" Sounding more like himself, Amari knows she can trust the conversation that's about to go down. She relaxes, glad to hear the coldness out of his tone all of a sudden. Allah wants to talk business. Not about earlier.

Amari sighs and sags. "You sound more like yourself. I guess I can give you that."

"I have always been myself." Allah snaps. "It's my wolf. Ragnar!" Allah spats in anger. He gives away the only clue that Amari needs. Ragnar has run off. Or gone dormant. Hopefully, it stays that way for a while.

Amari shakes her head. She shouldn't be thinking that way! Allah deserves to be armed with his wolf!

"Now." Allah sets a signed paper aside. "Let's talk business."

"We could've done this in your office." Amari defends herself.

"I don't wanna talk in my office."

"It's soundproof."

"But I want my pack to hear this conversation. They need to know I've made my final decision."

Amari winces as she starts to get the idea. The mate marks. Allah wants his pack to know the mate marks were an accident. Amari blinks.

"Go on," she drags out.

"I don't want the mate mark. And neither do you. Now, even though it's going to pain Ragnar when he comes back."

"You got in a fight with him about this." Amari interrupts Allah. "Didn't you?"

"I didn't want the mate mark, Amari! And I only gave it to you because Ragnar took over and left me with no control!" Allah turns around with a small stack of papers and he starts for Amari, looking at them. "This is everything you need for Madison's crowning."

Amari winces at the sudden change in subject. Allah stops an arm's length away from her and hands the papers to her.

"You have my consent," he says plainly. "But don't take it lightly. This is a serious change for me."

Amari nods her head then takes the papers from Allah and looks at them, scanning them for the key words.

*Madison Glenn Billow, rightful heir to Hell's Fire.*

With the words staring Amari in the face, she knows that she somehow got Allah to change his mind. Is he maybe trying to apologize and make up for earlier? She needs to do the same thing. She overreacted. She's under a lot of stress and the only way she can relieve it is by seeing Garrett in person, again.

Garrett. Oh, Amari misses him. Her heart starts to ache for him. For his touch and the sound of his voice. She wants to kiss him and let her cares float away while she stays in his embrace.

"Amari, I have to apologize for earlier," Allah grumbles, breaking the silence. "I was under the influence of Ragnar and it will not… happen, again. I can promise you that."

Amari looks up at Allah to notice the apologetic look on his face with his eyes soft.

"He thinks he can just have you." Allah looks down at the floor. "I tried to tell him it's not that easy."

"Well, the mate pull doesn't help," Amari says softly. "I mean… Right now, I just wanna…" Amari clears her throat, trying not to make it so awkward or weird. "Take care of you."

"Me too, Amari," Allah says with his hands behind his back. "I wanna take care of you and defend you. You're our queen. And the rightful heir to Hallam. I shouldn't be so hard on you. You've been training for this your whole life."

Amari nods her head. "I have you to thank for that. No matter how much of a pain I've been to you. Or you to me."

Allah snorts. "Well, let's not think about the past. It'll only get us into more trouble."

Amari's mouth opens, her lips slightly parted in shock. He doesn't mean… Oh, he means it. With the love in Allah's eyes suddenly Amari knows he's been thinking about the past ten years of Amari's dreams. All the walks in their gardens late at night when he couldn't sleep, the times they've been in her office going over business with a nice meal brought to them by Ada, the war with Kera when they fought side by side for a moment in perfect harmony as if they could read each other's mind, and the one intimate night they had together when he was grieving the loss of his first wife.

He made the first move and they were interlocked together a moment later with him deep inside of her. They both agreed it was because of his grief and he just needed something else on his mind after he marked Ada. They never revisited that moment again.

Allah clears his throat and brings Amari back. What is she doing? She's madly, irrevocably in love with Garrett and yet she's reminiscing to all the times with Allah!

"Anyway," Allah says in his business tone. "You have no need to worry anymore. Just… Don't have sex with my wife, again."

"Sorry, Allah." Amari lifts her chin and meets Allah's gray-eyed glare. "But, she's my mistress. So, it's gonna happen from time and time, again."

Allah stops a growl that starts in his chest.

"But thank you." Amari motions the papers in her hands, letting Allah see them for a quick moment. "I'll take these to Garrett first thing in the morning."

"Nonsense. I'll send a messenger." Allah turns and starts for his mini bar. "You just need to sign them as our queen. And you're staying here in the safety of my kingdom for one more day."

"Allah, I have to go."

"Not in that dress," Allah orders as he pours himself a glass of brandy, at his side bar. "And you're not leaving until tomorrow night as you planned. I won't let you go off schedule."

"And if I refuse to obey your order?" Amari turns to face Allah, putting the papers in front of her and grabbing her wrist with her free hand. She lifts her chin in a confident challenge.

Allah looks at Amari with his glass of brandy in hand, that teasing seductive look he gets when he's about to tease her. "My bed is open," he teases seductively. "You're welcome and free to get underneath me." He's completely himself!

Allah once made that joke just moments before Amari was doing exactly that! She presses her lips together in an attempt to keep herself from saying something snarky. Allah starts to giggle at her and it feels good to hear it.

"Don't get horny, now. You got a boyfriend that you love."

"You said it before I could." Amari winks at Allah then opens the door to walk out.

"Oh, and Amari."

Amari stops and looks around the doorframe to look at Allah.

"I'm sorry. Again."

"Me too. I overreacted earlier."

Allah shakes his head. "You had every right to. Ragnar was being an ass and could only think about marking you while I wanted a different release for him."

"Next time, lead with that. And we could've continued where we left off. I'm happy to help."

"You wanna," Allah starts in a teasing seductive tone. He motions at his bed, his eyes on Amari. "Get in my bed and start where we left off?" He flirts.

"You don't have your wolf anymore. It's not necessary."

Allah gives Amari the one minute as he finishes his brandy. After a moment he sets his glass down, making a sound of refreshment. "Well, again. I'm sorry."

Amari dips her head in a thank you then walks out of Allah's bedroom. She closes the door behind her then presses her back into it, letting out an exhale. She lays her head back against the door. She keeps telling herself she's not in love with Allah and that she just owes him a lot. He's trained her to be the goddess Hallam needs her to be. And she wants to rule her world like Allah rules his kingdom.

He's an amazing god of the were-kind and an amazing lycan king. His only problem is being overprotective and bullheaded. So much so he just about got himself killed by Viggo, who was wanting to take Allah's little sister to wife. The marriage never happened, Amari having to step in to make Viggo back off. She promised him that he would marry a woman that's worthy of his affections. And his loyalty.

In a way, Amari has picked up some of Allah's traits. Being overprotective is one of those traits. She gets that way with all of the creatures she's created here in Hallam and her friends and family back home. She also gets protective of Garrett and all of her maids, manservants, butler, and housekeeper. Amari feels a mind link prodding her and it's an all-too familiar one.

The smell of cedarwood and fresh ocean air hits her mind and Amari lets the love of her life in.

*Amari. Baby.* Garrett sounds lonely. *How are you?*

*Missing you…* Amari takes a moment with her boyfriend.

*I miss you, too, beautiful.*

A small smile spreads on Amari's face. *How was your day?*

*Uneventful for the most part.* Garrett sounds like he's busy with something. *But we saw a spiritwalker a few hours ago. It warned us of a war then walked away. I made eye contact with it and it didn't attack us.*

Amari lifts her head from the door and opens her eyes, something unsettling sinking into her gut. She doesn't like the sound of that. *That's unusual.*

*That's what we thought, too.*

*Did it say anything else?* Amari presses.

*Yes. You and Madi need to be crowned. Sooner than later.*

Amari shakes her head. *Garrett, you know that's not gonna happen. We can't risk it with Kera out there.*

*It knows that. But it still insists.*

*Could it maybe be working with Kera? Wanting to put us in danger?*

*Why would it, Amari? It works and hunts alone. It doesn't take any bargains. And it let us live after hearing and seeing us!*

*Because it had a message to deliver, Garrett!* Amari sighs and sags. *I don't wanna fight. I just wanna be in bed. With you.*

*And you will soon, Amari. I love you.*

*I love you more. Sleep well.*

*I will. And I want you to sleep well, too.*

Amari nods her head. *I'll meet you in our dreams tonight. If you'd like.*

*I'd love that, baby. Good night.*

*Good night.* Amari doesn't sever the mind link and neither does Garrett. It stays open. Even when Garrett finally falls asleep an hour later.

∞

Amari cuddles in with Garrett, entangling her leg with his and laying her head on his chest. She's grateful to be able to do this. But she so wishes she was with him in person.

Garrett moans and presses his lips into Amari's head. She knows what he's thinking. He can't wait for the day he can crown her. She can't wait either. Amari sighs and relaxes into Garrett.

"Amari," Garrett says lowly.

"What?" Amari mumbles, keeping her eyes closed.

"Think you can do something for me?"

"What?"

"If… Something happens."

Amari looks up at Garrett and her eyes meet his eyes. "Don't," she warns him. "Don't go there."

Garrett sighs and sags. He kisses Amari's head. "I know you don't want me to. But if something happens… Please choose wisely. Viggo is your best option, but I want you to keep Klauss in mind as well. Even though he has a wife already."

Amari sighs and sags, her brown eyes on Garrett's gray eyes.

He shakes his head. "I can't think of anyone else that would be better to rule by your side."

Amari kisses Garrett. "I can think of someone," she says softly into his lips. "And he's not going anywhere."

Garrett's hand trails up Amari's back. "I don't plan to." He rolls on top of her and looks at her. "I promise you I'm not going anywhere. But I'm still not superhuman like you."

Amari smiles. Then she rolls on top of the man she can see herself marrying and having a life with. She straddles him and lets her hair fall down around her face. "I can make you that way very easily."

"Oh," Garrett chuckles. "I know."

Amari kisses Garrett, holding his face in her hand. "I love you, Garrett Galaway. Irrevocably. And I'll always protect you and be by your side. I promise."

"Amari, I feel the same way. I'm making that promise as well."

Amari kisses Garrett then lies down next to him. They wind up cuddling and reminiscing through the whole night, talking about whatever comes to their minds.

∞

Garrett gets woken up abruptly and he's pulling the knife out from underneath his pillow as he gets dragged out of his tent by the ankle.

Fuck! He forgot to close the flap! Garrett looks down at what has him and he cuts the vine off of his ankle. He immediately gets up and rushes over to his tent as his team shoots at the titan spiritwalker. Not happening! He's keeping his promise to Amari!

Garrett grabs his gun from his tent, but he gets dragged by the ankle, again. What the hell?! Garrett spins onto his back and starts shooting at the titan spiritwalker, which is in the form of a massive treewalker. The spiritwalker lifts Garrett up in the air and he uses his core to lift himself up and shoot at the thing's face.

He gets a bullet in its eye and it lets out an earsplitting screech, making all life nearby cringe at it. The spiritwalker stabs one of its vine-like limbs into Garrett's side and he screams in pain. Unable to hold himself up because of the pain, he hangs from the spiritwalker's hold.

An all too familiar medium-tone female voice laughs evilly.

"You think it's that easy to kill a titan," the woman asks, her voice echoing next to the spiritwalker.

Garrett looks ahead to see he can see a village not too far from here. The spiritwalker spins him around slowly and he looks up at the witch, who is using her power to float next to the creature.

"Kera." He acts surprised to see her. "Son of a bitch, you look well. Looking twenty-five and younger every day. How do you do it? Is it wrinkle cream? Or… What do you use?"

"Oh, stop with the sweet talk. We both know you don't mean it."

"Do you wanna know what I really mean?"

"Like your opinion matters. Where's Amari?" Kera presses, impatient as ever as she cuts to the chase.

Garrett shrugs his arms dangling above his head with his gun in hand. "I don't know. Last I knew her estate."

Kera laughs sarcastically. "You think I'm stupid? I've already checked there just to find it abandoned except for two sisters fucking like there's no tomorrow."

Garrett furrows his brows in worry. "What'd you do with them?"

"Well, I didn't let them get away. They would've run home to let their king know that the witch is out and looking for revenge."

"Well, ain't that the truth. Now, put me down. And we can talk like real adults."

"No need. Just tell me where Amari is and I'll be on my way."

Garrett shrugs. "She's got so many places to hide I don't know which one she's at." Garrett gets stabbed in the side, making him close his eyes in pain.

"Start talking!" Kera snaps. "She doesn't deserve to be crowned as the goddess of Hallam! It gets to stay godless for once!" Kera threatens Garrett with her powers over the spiritwalker.

He shakes his head as he looks up at the witch, willing to sacrifice himself to keep the love of his life safe. "Sorry. But that's all I know."

Kera looks at the spiritwalker. "Kill him. He's of no use to us if he's not going to talk."

Garrett pulls his dagger out and the spiritwalker stabs him in the gut. He can hear Amari screaming for him and crying out, begging him to stay with her.

*Amari… I'm so sorry.* He mind links with Amari. He hears her cry out to him in pure fear and grief and his heart breaks for her.

Garrett throws his dagger at the spiritwalker's neck and it drops him on his head, making him lifeless.

# 16

Amari stares at the plate of food in front of her. She can't eat. Not after this morning. He's… He's gone! The love of her life… The man she wanted to crown her and be by her side…

Amari came rushing out of the bedroom in just a nighty early this morning while it was dark out, screaming for vengeance as tears streamed down her face. Allah caught her in the entry way and held onto her, telling her that it will eventually be okay. Her nails dug into his skin so deep she drew blood. He tried to soothe her, dressed only in boxers. But she didn't listen and tried to get to the witch.

Of course, he was able to stop her and put her back to sleep by using the mate bond to calm her down. Kera is *not* going to live this time! Amari is killing the cunt herself! A familiar female hand wraps around Amari's left forearm and Sirena gives her a reassuring squeeze.

Knowing what Amari is going through, Sirena has been by her side all day. Amari hasn't been wanting to see

Allah. And she doesn't want to look at him, now. Sitting to his left at the dinner table, Amari keeps her eyes on her untouched plate of food.

She hasn't been able to eat all day. Sirena pushes her chair back and she starts to rub Amari's shoulders. She puts her lips to Amari's ear.

"Let's go get ready," Sirena whispers, giving up on trying to get Amari to eat. "We're leaving super early."

Amari nods her head and she gets up, feeling Allah's eyes on her. He stands up with her.

"Amari," Allah mumbles. "Please." His hand lightly grips Amari's elbow. "Call for me if you need anything. I'm here."

Amari nods her head, keeping it low, and she walks away with Sirena. They start for the east wing as Sirena keeps her arm around Amari's waist, keeping her close and comforted. Sirena has helped Amari with the simplest things today. Brushing her teeth, brushing her hair, and getting dressed. One of Allah's omegas helped Amari get clean after balling in the shower for what seemed to be an hour, letting the water run cold.

She can hardly look at herself in the mirror either, knowing that all she'll see is a reminder of someone else. That someone being a complete asshole when he let his wolf take over. Even though he's apologized to her for his wolf's actions, she can't stand to think about him. But then again… He might be a good distraction for once.

Amari closes her eyes and shakes her head, standing in the middle of the bedroom in the east wing. No! She can't think like that! There's no way she can betray her boyfriend like that the day he passed away! A few knocks sound on the door and Sirena opens it.

"Allah, she can't," Sirena starts.

"I can feel her distress as my own," Allah cuts Sirena off. "And it's just as bad as when I lost Selena. Maybe even worse. Please, just let me try."

"She doesn't want to see you, Allah."

"She doesn't have to look at me. Just… Please, Sirena. It might calm her."

Sirena sighs behind Amari after a moment. "Fine," she growls. "But make it quick. She doesn't have long."

"Of course."

Sirena leaves Amari alone in the room with Allah and the door closes after a moment. Amari blinks, frozen to her spot. If she has one moment of weakness, she's going to be all over Allah. And that's not good for her. She can't give into him. No matter how bad she wants the distraction.

She can't go through this, again. Losing the love of her life. She shudders. Allah slowly approaches Amari from behind and he touches her elbow. The touch sends comforting waves through her body and she finds herself turning around and throwing herself at Allah, bringing his lips down to hers and desperately clinging onto him. He kisses her and holds her neck tenderly, entangling his fingers in her hair. He sends more comforting waves through her body from the touch and her mind screams for more.

Amari unbuckles Allah's belt. She quickly gets to his limp member, undoing his pants and pulling it out. He pulls away from her instantly and takes a few steps back away from her, a pained and confused look on his face.

"Mare," Allah whispers. "What are you doing?"

"I'm," Amari starts. She takes a step back. "I'm sorry." She looks down at the polished wood floor, ashamed. "It was just…"

"The familiar comfort of the mate bond," Allah finishes for her. "I… Understand. It's no wonder why we did it when I was grieving the loss of Selena."

Amari looks at Allah, broken inside. "You had a week to mourn before we…"

"I know." Allah gets close to Amari and brushes her bangs back, letting his fingertips brush her temple and send more comforting waves through her. "Which is why I'm confused as to why you want to do it so soon."

Amari lifts her chin. "Because the mate bond is comforting me in ways that I want more of it."

Allah leans in and kisses Amari. Their lips melt together and it turns tender. He holds her chin with his thumb on the nub, his finger underneath her chin. "I'm sorry," he whispers into her lips. "But we can't. Not like this."

Amari nods her head and pulls away, looking down at the floor. "Then I want you to leave."

"Mare," Allah starts, sounding heartbroken.

"I said leave," Amari snaps, glaring up at the man that she just barely started to consider as her husband and God. But she's not so sure she can go through with that choice. Garrett made her promise. "Allah."

Allah winces and his eyes show a broken heart.

"It's either you stay here and comfort me with the mate bond or you turn around and walk out that door, never to see me again."

Allah shakes his head, tears in his eyes. "You're in mourning. You don't mean it." He moves in and kisses Amari's forehead, using the mate bond to comfort her.

But it infuriates her this time instead. "I said leave!" She screams, thrusting him off and taking a step back away from him.

Allah sighs and sags, keeping his eyes on Amari. "I'll see you in Washington," he whispers. He turns around, rearranging himself then doing his pants back up and buckling his belt.

He walks out the door and closes it behind him, leaving Amari to break down for the tenth time today.

∞

Viggo uses his sword as he makes Amari Goddess of Hallam, settling it on one shoulder and then on the next.

He sheathes it after a moment and continues with the ceremony. He does his best not to look over at the man that left a mark on Amari, not very happy with him. The moment Viggo looked at Amari he knew something happened with Allah. He can see right through Ada's magic on the mate mark and it was bright as day.

The death of his best friend reached him in a mind link once Amari was close enough to him. Viggo's heart broke and he wished he spent more time with the man. He was like a brother to Viggo. Viggo looks at Amari as she stays on her knees with her head bowed.

"Queen Amari," Viggo starts. "Have you made a decision about your future husband and god?"

"I have," Amari replies.

"And who do you choose?" Knowing who she's going to choose, Viggo doesn't worry. He just glances at Klauss, who is wearing a crown as the prince of the takals. He may already have a wife, but takal princes and kings are known to take a second wife. And Amari would choose him in a heartbeat with Garrett now gone.

"Viggo."

Viggo looks at Amari in disbelief as she starts to say his full name.

"Amar. Grimert." Amari looks up at him and their brown eyes meet.

"Wait," Allah starts from the side, only a potential suitor because of the mate mark. "Viggo, if I must."

Viggo puts his hand up to silence Allah. He can't let the man have a word in. Allah will just ruin it! "This is your choice?" Viggo has to ask Amari this. It's part of the ceremony.

"Yes. I, Amari Rose Greenwod, choose you, Viggo Amar Grimert."

"Amari, wait," Allah speaks up. Viggo stops his objection with his hand out towards him and a warning glare.

"As my future husband, god, and fated mate." Amari adds that last part to show Allah who she would actually be mated to if takals had fated mates.

Takals are one of the very few creatures of Hallam that don't have fated mates. And they're one of Amari's creations.

"And I, Viggo Amar Grimert, accept you, Amari Rose Greenwood." Viggo brushes Amari's cheek lovingly with his chocolate brown eyes on her, happy to be the one she chooses. But he's also thrown off by her choice. He thought she would choose her best friend! "As my future wife, goddess, and fated mate."

Amari lifts her chin and lets her brown eyes keep eye contact with Viggo.

"As your officiant." Viggo cups his hands in front of him and summons Amari's gold crown with emerald-green jewels on it. "I pronounce you, Amari Rose Greenwood." He sets the crown on her head and it sits there proudly. "Goddess. Of Hallam."

"Amari, wait," Allah tries to object, again. But it's too late.

Viggo continues with the final decision. "With Viggo Amar Grimert as your rightful suitor, husband, and god."

Allah is heard on the side, shuddering an exhale of heart break. He lost the privilege to speak up when he interrupted Amari. She bows her head in respect and Viggo does the same. She instantly gets up and they hug as Sirena claps quietly from behind Amari.

Viggo kisses her cheek. He deliberately made the crowning low profile in a small clearing in the woods so Kera would never find out. Now, the only one that needs to be crowned is Madison. But Viggo can't crown her just yet. He doesn't have the authority.

Viggo puts his lips to Amari's forehead and holds her close. Amari saved Klauss. She and Viggo know Klauss has a wife back home that he wants as his queen. She's his everything.

Viggo rests his forehead on Amari's, wishing they could have their wedding now. But he knows that they both want to have it after this war is over.

"It's time to go," Viggo whispers.

Amari nods. "Then let's."

Viggo takes Amari's hand and leads her away from the clearing. Sirena hugs both of them as they try to pass and Viggo is happy for the quick distraction. She congratulates the mourning couple, wishing them the best in life. Viggo wraps one arm around Sirena and speaks low in her ear.

"I'll see you out at sea."

Sirena nods her head. Viggo pulls away from her, gently leading Amari over to their horses. He knows he doesn't need to. But he helps her mount her Friesian horse then he mounts his Friesian horse. They ride in silence for most of the way.

Viggo watches Amari, noticing she's different as she mourns the loss of her first choice and love of her life. Dressed in a white skew neck long slim dress with accents of gold lace, she looks absolutely dazzling. And like a goddess. She deserves the best and Viggo hopes that he'll be able to be that for her someday.

Amari catches Viggo staring at her as they draw near to the village he lives in. They keep eye contact as she lifts her head, her brown eyes soft and in mourning for the loss of her best friend.

"Thank you," Amari starts. "Viggo. I wouldn't have been able to go through with the crowning without you."

"Garrett trained me," Viggo replies lowly, giving Amari a comforting side smile. "We were about to go into coronations for Hell's Fire when he…"

Amari nods. "I think I might know a way so you can be an officiant for that as well."

"Well," Viggo drags out. "There's you."

Amari shakes her head. "I can't do that one to be honest." She confesses. "It's not in my field as Goddess of Hallam. It's you, the God of Hallam, that has to do that one."

Viggo nods. He looks down at his saddle for a moment. "When do you…" He clears his throat. "Wanna start planning?" He clears his throat, again, feeling like he's got a frog in his throat.

"The moment we get on the ship. If that's okay."

Viggo looks at Amari. "Yes, of course. We can do that."

Amari nods her head then looks ahead. "This village is bigger than the others."

"Well, we got a lot more people." Viggo looks ahead as he and Amari enter the village. People start congratulating Amari and Viggo at the sight of their clothing. They thank the people with a dip of their chin as they pass.

Viggo looks over at Amari when one of the women asks her who she chose to see she has her lips pressed together, biting back her tears. Realization hits everyone as they realize Amari was going to choose Garrett and they all start apologizing for his death.

One woman goes as far to offer Amari a prayer together for Garrett's safe passage to Heaven's Light. Amari looks at her with tears in her eyes.

"Thank you," Amari whispers as the horses stop for a treat given to them by a merchant selling fruit. "But I know he's there. I made sure he got there. Thank you, though."

"Of course," the woman says softly. She squeezes Amari's hand reassuringly. She takes a step back and lets Amari and Viggo go.

They quickly realize that everyone followed them to the docks. Amari turns around on her horse to look at everyone as Viggo gets down from his horse and hands Jorgan over to Kim once they reach the docks.

"Thank you, everyone," Amari starts, speaking up so everyone can hear her. "I appreciate your kind words and support. We made the coronation small, so Kera didn't catch wind of it and try to stop it. She killed my first choice, Garrett, thinking that with him gone there would be no crowning for me and Madi. But I can assure you Viggo has the power to do such crowning's. But we wanna keep that secret. Please, do *not* tell anyone." Amari looks around before continuing. "I know you're wondering who I chose since the love of my life is no longer with us. And I chose Viggo!"

Whispers of excitement gets around the people of the village, letting Viggo know they're staying quiet for Amari, wanting their goddess and future god to live.

"I can't thank you guys enough. You will be safe as long as Viggo and I rule together! I love you! May your paths be bright." Amari gets down from her horse and hands Laney to Kim. She looks up at the tall man in front of her. "Thank you, Kim. I appreciate you."

"And I, you," Kim replies. He leans over and kisses Amari's cheek. "Have a safe passage."

"Thank you." Amari walks over to Viggo and he offers her his arm. She takes it and they start for his battleship.

"Congratulations, Goddess Amari," one of Viggo's men speaks up. "We are happy to have you as our goddess and to fight beside you."

Amari nods her head. "Th-Thank you." Surprised, she looks up at Viggo as they continue walking. "You found a few men?"

"I found all of my men after the first war," Viggo replies, looking at Amari. "It only took a couple years, but I eventually found them. They were hiding in rocks like the cave men they are." He jokes lightly, making Amari laugh. It feels good to hear her laugh under the circumstances.

"Congratulations. That's a job well done." Amari pats Viggo's arm and he stands aside to let her walk up the plank to his ship first.

He follows her up. He makes a few orders for his men that are on the ship. After everyone is on their ship they sail off. Viggo walks over to Amari when he finds her after a few moments, finding her leaning into the side of the ship and looking out at the ocean.

"My lady," Viggo starts. "Care to join me in our chambers? I know how you must be tired."

Amari looks up at Viggo. "Yes. Well… How 'bout those plans?"

"Of course." Viggo dips his head to the woman he's loved for so many few years, now. He can't wait to get started in actually loving her after they've had time to mourn their loss.

∞

Allah gets out of the shower and wraps his towel around his waist. He should've fought harder for Amari. But he couldn't with Viggo shutting him up so much.

Allah knows when to shut up when Viggo is around. One hand movement from Viggo to stop you from talking and you obey the order. Or you regret ever saying anything at all. Allah is lucky after his few attempts, but he stopped after it was too late. He grips onto the sink and leans into it, trying to find the strength to continue his day.

In the kingdom of the Odinfah Lycan King, Allah has got to be careful not to break anything. That includes the omegas. Allah can't touch them even if he wanted to. But he won't put Amari through that pain, again. She didn't deserve it! That was a complete misunderstanding and Allah doesn't want to mess up, again!

Allah tries to steady his breathing, his eyes closed with his head hanging. What is he going to do? He just got news in a letter that Amy and Lexi are dead! His favorite omega… Gone! His Beta's wife Allah didn't know about… Gone! But to find out that the girls have been lesbians all this time! How did Allah let that slip his mind?!

He growls at the thought of fucking a lesbian. He most definitely won't do that, again! Ada was enough! Allah is strictly straight and he has a hard time with people that are not. He banishes them from his kingdom!

Allah tightens his grip on the sink and he instantly regrets it. He hears the sink crack and doubts fill his mind. Shit… He's going to get in trouble for this! And pay for the damage!

"King Allah," an omega says as she comes in. "I'm so sorry to disturb you. But King Mahal wants to speak with you."

Allah nods his head. It's about time he talks to his brother. He pushes off of the sink and strides into the bedroom. He quickly gets dressed for the day and then makes his way to Mahal's office. It doesn't take long and soon Allah is letting himself in with a few knocks on the door.

He finds Mahal at his desk with an omega and they're going over some paperwork. If Allah treated *his* omegas well, Mahal treats his omegas even better! He's always teaching his omegas a thing or two in politics if they're interested.

Allah stands in place with his hands in front of him, one hand clasping the wrist of the other, and he clears his throat. Mahal looks up at him.

"Brother," Mahal replies. He gets up and walks over to Allah. They hug briefly then get down to business. "I'm so sorry about your omegas. They truly deserved better."

"Thank you," Allah replies.

"Does Amari know?"

Allah shakes his head. "No. But I wouldn't want her to know anyway. She's not exactly a fan of mine right now."

"If it has to do with that mate mark, I wouldn't be surprised if Ragnar left you." Mahal points at Allah's mate mark then lets his hand fall.

Allah clears his throat. It sounds like he needs to get his mate mark covered, again! "I made him go for a run. He hasn't come back yet. And I prefer it as of right now. He hasn't been thinking clearly."

"Oh, so it was *his* decision to mark her!" Mahal doesn't sound surprised. But his eyes give away his laugh he's holding back. His wolf is probably laughing with him.

"Yes. Amari and I never felt that way about each other. But when she was releasing me from my pain, she accidentally marked me. After we made an agreement not to do that and keep it secret."

"So, Ada broke the mate bond."

"First. Yes. I wasn't very happy about it." Allah takes a deep breath in. "And I'm still not. I want her back more than anything in the world. Even, though…" He shrugs. "You know."

Mahal nods his head. "I can only imagine. You only have bad luck with women like her."

"Women like her are a disgrace," Allah snaps. "Even though I was in love with her and only want the best for her." Allah shakes his head in disgust. "Being gay just isn't right." He spats.

"This is why I'm the least favorite." Mahal jokes.

Allah narrows his eyes at Mahal. He knows Mahal supports the community because of his luna. Most of her family is gay and she's the only one that came out straight.

"But anywho." Mahal trails off and walks over to his desk. He takes a file from his omega and thanks her for it, calling her sweetheart. Mahal walks back over to Allah and hands him the file. "You've been asking for this for quite some time, now."

Allah stares at the file in awestruck disbelief.

"Your wife's death. And who's behind it."

Allah takes the file and opens it. The first thing he sees is a picture of him and Selena hugging and smiling at the camera.

"And why your pack just left her behind."

"Thank you, Mahal. I… I can't thank you enough for this. How did you… Get this information?"

"I have the best spies. And I placed a few in your own pack. They got to the bottom of things."

"I don't know what else to say." Allah looks at his brother, at a comfort to finally find out what really happened.

"Don't mention it." Mahal says sweetly, his hands in his front pockets. "It's the least I can do."

"I owe you one."

"Well, get home. Sleep. Relax. I can take care of the war from here."

"But Amari…"

"Is in good hands. And she made the right choice. You're not exactly God of Hallam material."

"But I trained her."

"To the best that you could."

Allah glares at his brother.

"Look. Nolan knew what he was doing with you and Amari. I'm not gonna lie. And while you're the god of all were-kind you're also the god of stupidity."

Allah winces. "Be careful, Mahal." He threatens. "I can easily take you down in a brawl."

"I don't doubt that. But you need to remember, Allah." Mahal shakes his head, looking up at his brother. "Amari is in control of Hallam and that includes you. She's the goddess of all gods and goddesses." He points at Allah then puts his hand back in his front pocket. "You need to tread lightly with her and you can most definitely learn a thing or two from her."

Allah clenches his jaw. He knows that. He's just too stubborn to listen.

"Just think about it." Mahal pulls away and walks over to his desk. "Go enjoy your day. I'll see you at an early dinner before you leave." He sits down behind his desk, where his little omega is waiting for him.

"Of course, Mahal. And thank you. I appreciate it."

Mahal looks up from his file on his desk and at his brother lovingly. "Don't mention it," he says softly.

Allah turns around with the file in hand and he leaves Mahal with his omega.

# 17

Amari pants as Viggo pins her to the deck and she tries to think about her next move. Trapped underneath him with her hands pinned above her head, she can only think of one move.

Training with him was a bad idea. He's much bigger than her! Amari thrusts her hips into Viggo, making him moan into her ear.

"Do it, again," Viggo growls seductively.

Amari laughs softly. There goes that plan! He's way too strong for her! What was she thinking going up against him? Viggo gets in between Amari's legs and he thrusts his pelvis into her, spreading her legs out wide. His men watch them.

Oh, now we're getting bold, are we? This isn't anything new to Amari. She's been in this cur bubble with Mike before! And she usually knows what does the trick.

"You can't get out of this. Admit it."

Amari snorts and she looks up at the man that's towering over her with his broad frame. Her breasts meet the top of his rib cage, Amari standing a foot shorter than Viggo. "Oh, I'll find a way."

"Let's see you try." Too tall to bend his head down to her ear since he's changed positions, Viggo decides to press himself against Amari and smother her face with his chest, wrapping his free arm around her.

She screams and laughs at his move. Classic for a huge man! Amari wishes she could bite Viggo's chest. But he has a thick shirt on that would make him not feel a thing. Amari is only left with one more thing to do. She bucks her hips into Viggo's hips and makes him rock back a little.

"Oh," Viggo moans, sounding like he's turned on. "Two can play at that game," he flirts.

Amari moves her head so she can bite Viggo's exposed bicep, clamping down on it.

"Ow!" He flinches, but he doesn't move, keeping her pinned.

Amari wraps her legs around Viggo's waist. She takes the moment to quickly slip out of Viggo's hold unsuspectingly and she wraps her arm around his neck as she rolls on top of him. As she rolls on top of him, she pulls out her dagger he gave her as a gift for their betrothal.

She puts it to his neck as she exposes it with her hand in his hair. On top of Viggo, Amari looks down at him. Their eyes meet and a grin spreads on his face.

He giggles at her.

"Oh, don't tell me you have another surprise," Amari retorts.

Viggo takes a quick glance down and then his brown eyes meet Amari's brown eyes. "Take a guess yourself." He flirts.

"Oh!" Knowing what Viggo means, Amari lets him go and slaps his chest. "Men." She gets up and Viggo stays down on the floor. Takals always have a comeback whether it's sexual or not. Amari can't help but shake her head.

"You know, at this angle you look like you've actually got some muscle," Viggo teases. "It's kind of surprising. Considering… You know."

Amari looks down at Viggo after putting her dagger away in its sheathe on her hip. "You better tread lightly," she drawls out in a teasing warning.

Viggo's eyes meet Amari's. "You're so tiny." He says in a cute voice. "Like a kitten." He enunciates the word 'kitten'.

"Oh!" Amari kicks Viggo's leg and he chuckles at her with a smirk on his face. Getting to know him the past five days has helped her with her grief. She feels as though she made the right decision, choosing Viggo instead of Allah.

Amari lends her hand to Viggo to help him up. He gladly takes it. But only to thrust her back down on him. Her breasts press into his chest and their brown eyes lock.

"Down here's better." He flirts, raising an eyebrow at his fiancé. His eyes land on her lips.

"You think you're so smooth."

"Aren't I?" He says lowly, looking into Amari's brown eyes.

Amari can't help but smile for the first time since Garrett's death, showing her pearly white teeth. "I'm pretty sure Garrett was better than you at being smooth."

Viggo's eyes shift to Amari's lips. "I guess I got a lot to live up to." He looks into her eyes.

"Just a couple things." Amari teases seductively.

"I guess I better get started."

Amari takes Viggo's hand and she helps him up as she gets up. But Viggo gives her some resistance, making her work to get him up. "You're seriously gonna make me break my back."

Viggo laughs and finally lets up, letting Amari pull him up. He gets close to her. "I'm tempted to break your neck and make you immortal." He flirts with her, knowing he can get away with it.

Amari throws her bangs back and looks up at the man she's slowly starting to fall in love with. She feels guilty for it, missing Garrett.

"You'll have to catch me first," she teases seductively.

Viggo pulls Amari into him and looks at her lips. "I just did."

Amari snorts. She looks at Viggo's lips then into his eyes. She so totally could kiss him. He's going to be her future husband and God after all! She might as well do what she wants to do.

Viggo leans in and his nose brushes against Amari's nose. The moment turns tender, Viggo resting his forehead on Amari's forehead. She knows what he's thinking. He wants to kiss her, but he's too afraid that it's too soon for her. She wants to kiss him. But she'd feel guilty for moving on from Garrett too fast.

A massive splash in the water is heard and a moment later a whale is calling out next to the ship. There once was a time Amari would have rushed over to look at the whale. But after an incident a few years ago she won't go near one. One of Viggo's men calls out.

"Land ho!"

Amari pulls her forehead away from Viggo's and she looks over to her right to find land appearing ahead. Amari can feel someone's presence on it. Someone dangerous and threatening.

∞

Adam walks out of the forest with his team and they're met by Amari and Viggo on the beach. They made it! Now, they can get down to business!

Adam walks over to Amari and they hug, letting his gun hang from his neck.

"I'm so sorry, Mare," Adam whispers. He presses his lips into the top of her head. "I was there when it happened."

"Did you," Amari starts, trailing off.

Adam nods his head. "His funeral was beautiful. Erika wished you and Mike could've been there."

Amari shudders in Adam's arms. "I wished I was there, too."

Adam takes a moment to reassure Amari before taking a step back and looking at her. "She's here. And she's stronger than ever. You're gonna need all the help you can get."

Amari nods her head. "We'll send word. Klauss and his army would be good reinforcements." She shakes her head and growls in disgust. "If only Madi was here. We could really use her and her wyverns right now."

Adam nods his head and looks down. "She's building a barrier as we speak. She hasn't gotten over here yet. But she will." Adam looks at Amari. "We're gonna need Amelia."

"I'll get word to her somehow as well."

Adam dips his chin. "Any news?"

"Viggo crowned me."

Adam blinks in disbelief.

"I am now Goddess of Hallam. So, I can fight with full power."

Chills run through Adam's body. He's so happy for her! And proud! "I wish it happened under different circumstances. But I'm still proud of you."

"Thank you."

Adam hugs Amari and gives her a reassuring squeeze. He looks between her and Viggo. "How did it go?"

"Well," Viggo puts in. "She chose me."

"Congratulations, man." Adam offers his hand to Viggo and they shake hands.

"Thank you. We're having the wedding after everything has calmed down."

"Good call."

Viggo pulls Amari into his side and he looks at her. "We think so, too."

"Just don't have a honeymoon baby," Adam teases. "Everybody will think you'll be covering it up with the wedding." Adam winks at Amari, who laughs.

"Oh, like you did?" Amari teases. "You know everybody still believes you and Maidene got pregnant before you even proposed!"

Adam scoffs a laugh. "That's because I'm that smooth."

"Oh, shut it." Amari slaps Adam's arm teasingly. "We'll send word where Kera is and then we'll wait. Once everyone gets here, we'll make a plan of attack."

Adam nods. "That works."

"Good work, Adam. You've really stepped up since Garrett's passing."

"Hey," Adam says softly, his voice barely loud enough for Amari to hear. "I got a lot to live up to. He led his team greatly."

Amari nods. "And you'll do the same."

Adam dips his head to his goddess. "Thank you." He looks at his new team and they wait for his command. "Let's keep an eye on her. Stay hidden while she puts up the barrier."

Adam's team nod their heads. He looks at Amari, who is watching him with Viggo's arm around her. "We'll keep you posted."

Amari dips her head. "Thank you, Adam."

∞

Amari walks out of the shower in just a towel as she French braids her hair. Her legs clean and shaved she feels better. She needed that shower. Viggo made her sweaty and stinky this morning with their training.

That man sure is full of himself. But not in a bad way. He doesn't think he's the strongest or the best. He just knows he can take on Amari with no problem. So, in training he pushed her to her limits. Which is a good thing.

Everything goes quiet on the ship as everyone retreats to their bedrooms. Then he's right behind her. Amari stops as she feels Viggo right behind her, his chest just barely brushing the back of her head. Amari hurriedly finishes her braid, knowing what he's thinking. And if he's not careful, it just might happen.

Amari ties her hair tie at the end of her braid as she turns around to look up at her fiancé. Their brown eyes meet, his darker than hers.

"Can I help you," Amari asks teasingly.

"Yeah," Viggo says softly. He leans in towards her, his nose barely brushing hers. "Stop tempting me."

"That's not my fault, you know."

Viggo chuckles with a smirk on his face. "Oh, but it is."

"How?"

"Well, look at you. You're wearing a towel with your hair freshly wet."

"I just got out of the shower."

Viggo puts his lips to Amari's ear as he gets a little closer to her. "No, shit, Sherlock," he whispers seductively. "And you showered without me."

Amari snorts and smiles at Viggo. Their eyes lock. "That's because you're too busy with your tribe." She teases.

Viggo moans and pulls Amari's hips into his. "I'm not, now."

Amari throws her bangs back and lets her brown eyes meet Viggo's brown eyes. Soft in the dim light, Viggo's eyes look dark with lust. He lets his hands trail up Amari's sides and they tug at her towel.

"One little slip," Viggo mumbles, his voice filled with passion and lust. "And I could be inside of you." He threatens with a soft tone.

Amari searches Viggo's eyes. "Then what's stopping you?"

Viggo rests his forehead on Amari's forehead. "You," he whispers, making Amari flinch.

"Why me?"

"Because I know I'm not the one you were hoping for."

"How can you say that?" Amari looks at Viggo's lips.

"You were all about Garrett." Viggo shakes his head as he lets his hands fall down Amari's sides and hold onto her hips. "And I don't want you to think that you have to rush into anything with me."

"Viggo…" Amari's heart breaks, realizing that Viggo is more of a gentleman than he made her believe.

"Take your time. I know you're not ready for me."

"That's not true," Amari tries to defend herself.

She wants him! Amari wants to feel Viggo all over her! She wants to feel his touch. His caress that excites her. His arms that she has always felt safe in wrapped around her and keeping her close. Amari wants to feel Viggo's lips on her, ravishing every single inch of her body and leaving her marks to claim her, showing anyone that dares to touch her that she's well taken care of and protected.

Amari can see herself in the morning, covered in hickeys from head to toe from the lovemaking she had with Viggo.

"Don't lie to me, Amari," Viggo warns lowly. "I don't want you to tell me what I wanna hear. Not when you don't mean it."

Amari gets on her tiptoes and she holds the back of Viggo's neck. She lifts her head, brushing her lips over his.

"I'm not lying," she whispers. "I want you." Amari makes the move, pressing her lips into Viggo's and kissing him softly.

It takes him a moment, but he opens up to her and kisses her. He wraps his arms around her waist and pulls her in close. Viggo swallows Amari, their tongues meeting in a passionate kiss. She holds onto him, her towel as the only barrier covering her body. If he wanted to take her, he could easily do it with just a flick of his wrist.

But Viggo pulls away after a moment, panting and gasping for air. He rests his forehead on Amari's and they stay in each other's arms for a moment. Viggo kisses Amari's forehead.

"I'll be in the shower," Viggo whispers into Amari's forehead. He leaves her standing in the middle of their bedroom, Amari still wearing just a towel, and he walks into the bathroom, leaving her dumbfounded and feeling like a fool.

What just happened?

# 18

A booming sound comes from the island and Amari jumps, looking towards the sound.

What was that? What just happened? Something *did* just happen, didn't it? Amari looks over at Viggo and their eyes meet. He gives her a knowing nod. It's time to go in.

Viggo lifts his hand and motions for the battleships to move in. It feels like it takes forever, the battleships sailing in towards the land with the motors off and depending on the sails. They don't want Kera to know that they found her.

Amari and Viggo get to the island quietly in an hour and race down the ramp. Their feet hit the sand and they push into the forest without hesitation. Viggo gets held back as some undead wolves attack him.

Kera.

Amari stops and helps, killing every wolf that comes after her and Viggo with her light sword. Viggo warns Amari about a gray wolf in her blind spot and she slices its head off as it lunges for her. The wolf turns into ash and then Amari and Viggo look around as it goes deadly quiet.

It's clear. They give each other a nod then push forward. It isn't until they get in the middle of the forest that they reach a clearing. Viggo and Amari stay hidden in the trees as they scout the area. Something's not right. This seems too easy!

Amari gets on high alert, keeping her eyes peeled. She doesn't want to miss a thing. Anything can happen in this scenario! Klauss is spotted across the way and Amari reaches out to him in a mind link as their eyes meet.

*It's about time you showed up,* Amari teases, a smirk on her face.

*I have a whole army to lead,* Klauss puts in. His blue eyes pierce Amari's brown eyes from across the clearing. *You try getting them going.*

*Alright, alright. Just don't slow us down… Old man.*

*I know someone older.* Klauss teases.

Amari snorts and bites back a smirk. *Have your men on the south side of the island. If Kera tries to make a run for it, which I highly doubt, we want to push her that way.*

Klauss nods his head and quietly slips away. A low, familiar feline growl sounds next to Amari and she looks at her companion behind her, Viggo scouting the area. What's Raja doing here?!

An earthquake occurs and Raja holds Amari steady, pressing into her side. This is a 2.7 magnitude by the feel of it. They're getting worse. Amari and Raja wait the earthquake out and then they move forward.

Kera comes out of the small house at the edge of the clearing, holding onto Mike by his short hair. Amari and Raja fall back as they watch Kera. She has Mike's arms tied behind him with rope and he has a nasty gash on his chest. Amari curses underneath her breath. He doesn't look good. She needs to get him somewhere safe!

"Not very many people can sneak up on me," Kera threatens, sounding impressed. "But oh, Amelia. It's good to have you on my side." Oh, she is so wrong on who's here!

Amari shifts the air and she turns it into a ball in her hand. She turns it into a plasma ball. The lightning inside of it lights up and Amari throws the ball into Kera. Kera gets thrown back, being thrust off of Mike and dropping him.

She flies into the wall of her house and Amari rushes over to Mike, who is bruised and cut up. Fuck! He's worse than she thought! Amari uses her dagger to cut Mike's ropes loose and she discovers he's barely holding on.

"No, no, no," Amari says lowly. She checks for a pulse on Mike. "Mike? Mike… Can you hear me?" Amari rolls Mike onto his back and she barely feels a pulse.

Something hits Amari in the shoulder and it gets dislocated. She looks up to see Kera back on her feet. Shit. Of course, no plan goes perfect. Why would they? This is a battle!

"Mike, if you can hear me," Amari starts as she turns towards Kera, standing up. "I'm getting you out of here. You're safe, now."

Kera throws a few daggers at Amari and Amari stomps on the ground to create an earth barrier in front of her while she puts her shoulder back in place. The daggers fly into the earth as it rises up and protects Amari. She then lets it fall back down and she summons one of her light daggers, throwing it at Kera. Kera uses her magic to disintegrate it into nothing before it can meet skin.

"Nice try, Amari," Kera spats. "But my powers are stronger than your little magic tricks."

"Then try to stop this," Amari growls threateningly. She summons fire into her hand and she throws a fire ball at Kera unexpectedly.

An arrow flies into Kera's shoulder, distracting her, and she looks for the culprit as the fire ball burns her neck. She growls a scream in frustration for being fooled so easily. Amari looks around the island to realize there's a portal here. And it goes right into a hospital.

While Kera is distracted by flying arrows and disintegrating them Amari twists her fist and she raises the palm of her hand, activating the portal that winds up being a few paces away.

Great…

Amari looks around for something to help her transport Mike while she holds the portal open and Raja unexpectedly puts him on her back, the ground moving like pixels. She rushes over to the portal and steps through, disappearing on the other side. Amari waits for Raja to return, holding the portal open.

She gets hit in the shoulder by something sharp and a moment later there's movement in the portal. Amari gets hit, again. A stabbing pain starts in her spine. Shit! Things are going down real fast! Raja leaps through the portal with a roar and her fur stands on end as she growls at Kera, prowling as if she's stalking her prey.

That's it, girl! Keep her distracted! Amari does her best to push through the pain and she turns around to face Kera.

"Shit's going down," Amari threatens in a growl. She closes the portal behind her and she summons her long whip. Here we go. Amari snaps her whip at Kera without warning and Kera gasps at the burning pain. Where she's a witch weapons from Heaven's Light burn her skin. Here, witches are considered evil. And they help Amari in the long run, burning witches and warlocks whenever they come across her.

Klauss and his army stay hidden in the forest as they wait for Amari's signal. They don't want to move in too soon. And by the looks of it, Amari has the upper hand at the moment.

Klauss keeps his eyes peeled, not wanting to miss a thing. He pays attention to his surroundings with his eyes on Amari, who's throwing a force of wind combined with fire against Kera. But Kera throws her own force of magic into it, meeting it in the middle. Something breaks a branch in the forest and makes Kera's gaze falter.

Amari takes the moment and throws a ball of fire at Kera's neck. She screams in frustration as the fire burns her. But she heals quickly with her magic. Amari uses her whip to snap at Kera and something shifts behind Klauss. He looks behind him and watches a titan spiritwalker stand up, horror striking him.

Fuck. This isn't good.

"Take cover," Klauss yells, ordering his army. "And fire at will!" Klauss calls on Layka, his grimmal, and she appears in just moments. He leaps onto her back as she flies by and they take to the sky. They fly around the spiritwalker with a good distance between them.

Layka fires at the spiritwalker as she flies past it and Klauss shoots an arrow at its soulless eye. It screeches in pain and looks for its attacker. But Layka goes into camouflage through a burning fire. Klauss and his army coordinate their attacks and try to stay out of reach of the spiritwalker.

In the form of a creature with a box head and a slim body, the spiritwalker truly looks terrifying. Its arms lash out at Klauss and his army, but they stay out of reach. A grimmal flies in and snaps on the spiritwalker's arm, taking a chunk out. Starting away from it, the grimmal races out of its arm length before it can grab her.

Another grimmal moves in with its rider on its back and the grimmal lands on the spiritwalker's back, digging its talons in and taking chunks of its body armor off and revealing its vulnerable skin. This is going to take a while, but it should work.

∞

Kera pants as she uses her powers to heal herself quickly. She glares at Amari. She somehow became the goddess of Hallam! But how?! Kera killed Garrett! She usually knows things like this!

Furious, Kera lashes out at Amari with her power and Raja blocks Kera's blow, protecting Amari. Raja lets her hair stand on end as she protects Amari and she growls at Kera. Fuck. This cat is going to be the death of Kera if not Amari's whip. She's got to be careful at how she strikes and defends, or Raja will tear her head off!

"Give it up, Amari," Kera barks. "I'm better than you in every way!" She lies. She knows what Amari is capable of now that she's at full strength. Who knows how this battle is going to end!

Nolan asked Kera to help him create this world. She did that! She may have used spells to quicken up the process of the making of the world, but she did it because Nolan asked her to! Now, everything is falling apart! This world is now corrupt, most of the spells gone. If the takals fix the axis with the help of the earth snakes, then there will be no spells left! And Kera will cease to exist. She can't let that happen! Hallam needs her! She needs this place! She met her husband here!

Amari shakes her head. "Think again," she growls threateningly. Amari lifts her palm at her side and Kera hears a rumbling.

What's going on? Kera throws a dagger at Amari and Amari burns it to ash before it can meet her neck. Kera looks over just before the ocean water envelopes her and she hears screeches in the water. Mermaids surround Kera and tear at her flesh. Trying to hold her breath, she screams inside of her head at every single sting that meets her torso.

Fuck! This isn't good! Why is it going this way?! One of the mermaids digs something into Kera's stomach and she screams in pain, unable to hold back any longer. Another stabbing pain in her gut and no more screams come out of her as she gasps for air. But water fills her lungs, instead.

Blood seeping from every pore, Kera tries to heal herself. But drowning makes her powers weaken and the mermaids continue to slash at her. Sirena swims in front of Kera and stabs her gut with a spear. Her purple eyes pierce Kera's brown eyes before the ocean water goes back to where it came from, the mermaids and Sirena going with it.

Kera is left trying to breathe in some air. But water is trapped in her lungs. She blindly looks up at Amari and with one more attempt she thrusts a few daggers at Amari. Raja uses her tail to get rid of them, but one hits Amari in the neck and she goes down on her knees.

Amari lashes her whip at Kera and it wraps around her neck. The pressure tightens around her neck and Kera is left with no chance to survive. The smooth skin of the whip digs into her skin and she can feel herself going. This is not how it's supposed to end!

The titan spiritwalker fights against Amari's creatures and Kera hears a few screams. The last sound she hears is Amari's best friend yelling orders before Amari rips Kera's head off of her shoulders with her whip, a glare on her face with vengeance.

Garrett.

∞

Viggo puts his sword away after killing the last of Kera's undead minions. A shift in the air and Viggo knows something's wrong. This kind of shift in the air has only happened once before. And it's never good.

"Amari," Viggo screams, scared for the worst of what's happened to the love of his life. He rushes over to the clearing and stops when he sees Amari lying on the ground, Raja crumbling in front of her and falling to her knees.

Raja shakes as she moans in mourning. Fuck… No! Viggo runs over to the woman he gave his heart to and he assesses her body. A dark, slim dagger is piercing her in the neck, hitting an artery. Her death. Viggo takes the dagger out of Amari's neck and Amelia is on his side immediately.

This is not happening… This is not fucking happening! There's only one thing to do! Something that only Viggo can do as Amari's rightful suitor and takal! Tafalas are heard coming out of the water and attacking the titan spiritwalker.

"Viggo," Ambroz calls.

Viggo looks up at his tafala as he quickly joins him. Their brown eyes meet. "Distract it."

Ambroz nods his head before slithering away and attacking the spiritwalker.

"I wanna make it happen," Viggo orders. He looks at the witch that has been good this whole entire time. "Heal her. Please." Viggo begs.

He's usually not one to beg. He's headstrong and stubborn! But when it comes to Amari… He'll beg for her life to be spared every time.

Amelia nods her head and uses her magic to heal Amari's death wound after taking the black dagger out of her neck, Amari in her arms. Moments later Amari has no wounds and bruises and she's back to normal. Now, for the tricky part. Viggo looks up at Raja as Amelia hands Amari back to him.

"Raja," Viggo asks. "You're the Heart of Hallam. I need your help."

Raja nods her head and steps forward.

"Amari," a concerned female voice yells.

A wyvern lands not far from Viggo and soon Madison is ripping Amari from his arms. He glares at her.

"Get your hands off her," Viggo snaps with a threat. He takes his beloved fiancé back. "And go home! You're going to throw Hallam off!"

"I am home!" Madison snaps, glaring at Viggo. He deepens his glare at her in confusion. "Garrett made me Goddess of Hell's Fire and I took care of things there before I made my way here. Let me do this!"

"You don't have the power!" Viggo retorts.

Madison looks at Amelia, ignoring Viggo. "Who are you?"

Amelia looks at Madison with a soft glare. "Amari's witch. Now, back off, Madison. You don't have the power to bring Amari back. Only Viggo can do this."

Madison stares at Amelia in shock.

"Take care of the spiritwalker," Amelia snaps. "That's where you can help!"

Madison nods. "I'll be back." She threatens lowly. Madison runs over and gets on her wyvern's back. They take flight and make their way over to the spiritwalker. They assess the creature before moving in and attacking it.

Viggo lays Amari down in front of him. He opens his arms and activates the life circle. Where he's her officiant, suitor, and a takal he gets to bring her back to life and bind her to Hallam. Amelia steps out of range of the life circle immediately and she watches from a distance, using her power to assist Viggo and making a barrier so no one can get through and disturb the process.

Candles appear at the rim of the life circle and Viggo speaks in Old Norse, his native language.

"I call upon my ancestors to watch over my goddess and bring her back to me. I sacrifice the life she once had in Homba and bind her here to Hallam with the permission of the Heart of Hallam. Raja of the South and West kings and queens."

Raja steps into the circle and she walks over to Amari, standing above her. Raja bows her head and blows her mystical breath on Amari, giving her new life. And a new meaning.

"As she breathes life back into Goddess Amari we bless her, Goddess Amari, with immortality. And the gift as our Goddess of Hallam. With full power and meaning."

The earth shakes as it starts to accept the new life as part of its own. Viggo keeps his arms open as he waits for a few minutes. Screeches of the war with the spiritwalker continue as the spiritwalker tries to fight against two tafalas, a wyvern, and multiple grimmals.

When the earthquake stops the circle and candles disappear. Viggo lays his hand on Amari's cheek to find warmth in it. He straddles her and waits for her to wake up, hoping the spell worked. He holds her face in his hands and when her eyebrows furrow, he kisses her with relief.

Amari's lips meet Viggo's in a kiss and her arms wrap around his neck. Good gracious! She's back! Viggo pulls Amari into a hug and holds her close. He moans into her ear.

"I'm so glad to have you back," Viggo mumbles.

"I'm glad to be back," Amari whispers, her chin on Viggo's shoulder.

"Let's get you home."

"I have something to do first."

Viggo gets up with Amari and she lifts herself in the air with her newfound power with the elements. Amari shifts her hands in front of her as she floats above Viggo and she lifts all the rocks in between her and the titan spiritwalker, which has been fighting its big and small opponents.

Phoenixes are heard and one comes towards Amari and Viggo, shifting into human form as his feet meet the earth. Henry. That's quite the entrance! Henry watches in admiration as Amari throws the rocks and some boulders into the spiritwalker to gain its attention, phoenixes moving in to attack.

Once the spiritwalker looks at her with its one good eye, she thrusts the arrow out of its wounded eye with a flick of her wrist and it screeches an earsplitting screech, crippling its opponents. Phoenixes attack its face, unfazed by its screech, and Klauss's men continue to fight once the screech stops, coordinating their attacks with each other and Madison.

Ambroz and two other tafalas clamp their jaws down on the spiritwalker, using their bodies to wrap around it. Their muscles are seen tightening around the creature to constrict it. Amari ignores the screech and she thrusts that same arrow that penetrated its eye into the spiritwalker's neck. She controls the arrow, thrusting it out of the spiritwalker's neck and back in, again, repeatedly, her creatures coordinating with her attacks.

She continues with her attacks until the creature crumbles and falls to the ground as Klauss and his army continue shooting their arrows into its neck, the tafalas unwrapping their bodies around it and letting it fall.

Madi's wyvern fires at the spiritwalker and burns its face before it finally meets the earth and doesn't pick itself back up.

# 19

Raja walks into her chambers and she gets greeted by her sons and daughters. They purr at her welcome.

Kishan, Lamesh, and Natiri chuff, butting their heads into Raja's flank in turn. She's grateful to be home. And to have all of her kids, biological and adopted, here with her. She moans as they smother her with loving rubs and soon she's knocked on her back. Raja looks up at them and Natiri rubs her forehead on Raja's forehead. They must have really missed her.

Raja rolls to her side, rubbing her forehead on Natiri's. It isn't until a few moments later Raja gets a breather from all of her kids. She looks over at Rain, who takes charge when she's not around. It's time. Raja gets up and meets with her oldest in the middle. They rub heads and chuff in unison.

Raja leads Rain into a room that's heavily guarded with guards and traps. Raja disarms all the traps and Rain follows her in. Raja looks back at her daughter and blinks slowly, turning her head to look at the emanating purple stone on the wall. The heart stone. The reason this world has a Heart. And always will.

∞

Amari puts the gold crown with red rubies on Viggo's head as he kneels in front of her and their people cheer for them.

Finally united as God and Goddess, Amari couldn't be happier. Just this morning they had their wedding ceremony. Here in the afternoon, Amari crowned Viggo as her God. And now, it's time to celebrate.

Viggo stands up and his eyes meet her eyes. He moves in and their lips crash into each other. It's done. When they're both now immortal it's going to be hard for them to die. They're a force to be reckoned with. And nobody dares to cross one of them when the other will be right there with their sword against the person's skin.

Viggo takes Amari's hand and he takes his place beside her as the crowd chants "Long live our God. Long live our Goddess." Amari smirks at the chant and looks up at the man that she so loves and their brown eyes meet. The green rings around her brown brighten up and she feels it.

Amari and Viggo make their way over to their chairs and they sit down in them, in sync. Viggo takes Amari's hand in his. He mind links with her.

*You should have had this,* Viggo starts. *You deserved a crowning like this.*

*Viggo, you know I'm more the type of having it small,* Amari replies. She looks at Viggo. *My crowning was perfect.*

Viggo's eyes meet Amari's. *Then we should've made the celebrations small.* He teases, making Amari snort and smile at him.

*There's only one celebration I can think of having right now and it is small.*

Viggo's eyebrow raises. *Please. Do tell.*

*It involves our bed.* Amari seduces.

Viggo growls in pleasure and he leans over, putting his lips to Amari's ear. "Don't tempt me, Mare," he seduces in a low tone. He nips her ear, leaving her wanting for more.

Amari turns her head, wanting to get back at Viggo. But he pulls his head away before she can do anything to him.

*Get back over here,* Amari seduces.

Viggo chuckles in Amari's mind, stirring her down there and making her hide her arousal. If the were-kind smells her arousal, she won't be able to pull away with Viggo without any suspicions!

*You're gonna have to wait, my love.* Viggo's voice echoes in Amari's mind and she finds herself clenching her thighs together.

Once everyone's chants die down, they get onto the celebration. Food is brought out by the cooks and maids and they celebrate with everyone else. People of all creatures come up and congratulate the couple at their chairs. It's a long line, making Amari mind linking with Sirena to ask her for some water for her and Viggo.

When Sirena reaches them Amari and Viggo are laughing at a lycan's story of his daughter crushing on one of Viggo's men, going as far as kissing him in the middle of the whole village and embarrassing the both of them.

"Funny thing is they're now engaged," the lycan says, ending the story.

Amari laughs in dumbstruck amazement and Viggo is laughing so hard his face is going red. His infectious laugh makes her laugh even harder to the point no sound is coming out of her mouth. Sirena hands the happy couple their glasses of water after the lycan congratulates them, again, then walks off.

"Thank you, Sirena," Amari says after regaining her composure. She takes the glass of water from her cousin, grateful to wet her parched throat.

"Yes," Viggo replies as he takes his glass of water. He clears his throat. "I was just about to ask one of my men in a mind link to get me some."

"Your wife beat you to it," Sirena replies, putting her hands in front of her and holding onto her wrist. She winks at Viggo.

"Thank you, wife." Viggo leans over and kisses Amari's cheek.

Sirena looks at her, her violet eyes gleaming. "Cousin."

Amari looks up at Sirena.

"I was hoping for a quick word."

"Anything, cousin."

"Matt and I are wanting to start the clean up a little early. So, you and Viggo can leave and have some time together. Just the two of you."

Amari nods her head. "How early?"

"In a half an hour."

Amari blinks a few times, dumbstruck. That's oddly soon! She looks at Viggo and their eyes meet. "What do you think? Do you wanna leave that early?"

Viggo shrugs. "We've been here for almost two hours, now. We might as well."

Amari nods her head at Viggo then she looks up at Sirena. "Fine. You have our permission."

Sirena smiles and dips her head. "Thank you, cuz."

Amari dips her head to Sirena. "Just don't push it with the lycans. They've been super nice and formal. But we both know they were hoping for their king to be by my side. I once bore his mark and he bare mine."

"Of course. I'll tread lightly with them."

"Thank you."

Sirena backs up then turns away. Amari looks over at Viggo and his brown eyes suggest what she's thinking.

*Amari,* a familiar low male voice says in a mind link with Amari. *Wait.*

Viggo's fingers curl into the armrest of his chair and his knuckles turn white. Did he hear that, too?

Fuck…

**Immortal Dreams Trilogy continues
with Mother of Dreams!**

**Buy your copy today!**

**Immortal Dreams Trilogy:**
Different Shades of Dreams
Mother of Dreams
Traitor of Dreams

**Find out what influenced Amelia in the prequel Amelia's Flaws!**

**Want to know what happens after the events of Mother of Dreams?**
Ada's Rule

**Find out the aftermath of Traitor of Dreams in Malech's Wrath!**

Want to read about another world? Check out the new series!

**Don't Forget Me Series:**
Dreamy Nights
My Dreams or Yours
Alechi's Mate
Raising Ashley
Abraxas' Fate